MAGICAL MURDER

LYON FOX MYSTERIES BOOK 1

ANN DENTON

LE RUE PUBLISHING

Le Rue Publishing
320 South Boston Avenue, Suite 1030
Tulsa, OK 74103
www.LeRuePublishing.com

ISBN: 978-0-9985437-7-2

To Jenn for her wedding.

May you have the most amazing happily-ever-after of all time.

The Lyon Fox Mysteries

Magical Murder - Book 1

Enchanted Execution - Book 2

Supernatural Sleep - Book 3

Hexed Hit - Book 4

Tangled Crowns Series

My first reverse harem series is the Tangled Crown series. It's a medieval fantasy with a bully romance feel in the first book.

Knightfall - Book 1

MidKnight - Book 2

Knight's End - Book 3

Lotto Love Series

My second reverse harem series is the Lotto Love series. Its a rom-com reverse harem with a private island, lottery money, and tons of handsome men.

Lotto Men - Book 1

Lotto Trouble - Book 2

Jewel's Cafe Series

Jewel's Cafe is a series of stand-alone reverse harem novels each written by a different author. My book is Ruby, the sixth title in the twelve book series. Ruby is the perfect mix of romance, heat, and comedy.

Ruby - A Reverse Harem Romance

Timebend

If you're in the mood for more intrigue, check out my Postapocalyptic Thriller series.

Melt - Book 1

Burn - Book 2

CHAPTER 1

"**F**ML. No seriously. Eff my life. Felony investigations gets a hot new supervisor and we're stuck with Grouchy McGrouch-Pants? Why do I still work here? Remind me."

I eye our supervisor with distaste. A crotchety fat werewolf named Arnold, he runs the misdemeanor unit at the Tres Lunas District Attorney's office—a quaint little magical community in Southern California. And he lives to make my life miserable. Case in point: he just dropped fourteen new files on my desk.

"Bella's out. Lyon, you get the new DUIs." He ignores my death stare and tromps off. "Arraignments in ten."

"I'm a paralegal, not an attorney!" I call after him.

"You're whatever I need you to be," he calls back, not even bothering to look.

He shuffles over the tiled floor and the door to his office thumps closed. I stick my tongue out, but quickly withdraw it. The stale stench of sweat fills the paralegals' room. Probably because they stuff about twenty of us in here. Ick.

I hate that, technically, Arnold's right. Night Court doesn't have the same ridiculous hoops as human courts. There's no stupid fill-in-the-bubble bar exam. There's the hot seat. Learning on the fly.

Since Bella's out, the assignment means Grouchy not only gave me her cases, he's also sending me down to handle tonight's arraignments. Just a listing of accusations and setting the next court date. But still. Then I have to deal with the pile on my desk...

"I'm quitting."

"I'd believe it if you didn't say it four times a day." My best friend, JR, leans forward over her desk adding a cover sheet to the new bite-and-run case she's filing. The only other paralegal in the office who's not part were-animal and perpetually out on leave for one of her sick cubs—she's my rock.

I tug at JR's bun. She's all into the librarian look at work. Dark glasses, brown hair up, frumpy blouses. As if that will keep the guys here from staring at her massive rack. She's half-nymph. Unfortunately for the guys, she's the world's most proper, sweet, and innocent nymph. No free-spirited hippie nymph stereotype for her. She's been with the same satyr for two years. Love, she calls it. Crazy, I call it.

"I'm gonna be here until noon again!" I grumble and lean against her desk, which, being a government issued piece of crap, squeaks in protest. JR, the consummate good-girl, ignores me and keeps working.

I scoot my butt closer to her workspace in an attempt to annoy her. "I can always just move in with you. No more rent. No more need to work here." I flutter my eyelashes to ensure she knows I am not at all serious. Her place is the world's tiniest apartment, which would never work for my…

"Your books would never fit Ly-Ly," JR says as she swats my hip, and leans over to get a paper clip. She clips her file and then grabs a pen to initial her work.

"Tell me you have to go downstairs to file that. Please." I'm jonesing for a coffee break.

JR smiles, "I have to go downstairs to file this … after I get it signed by Grouchy McGrouch."

I shudder. "You're on your own then. No way I'm going within fifteen feet of him."

JR stands and straightens her pencil skirt. "No. Wait? You don't like him?"

I shove her playfully.

She smiles. "Haven't seen the new guy yet. But I hear he's part dragon-shifter. Almost as good as a vamp." JR raises an eyebrow.

She likes to call me a vampophile. I'm a little obsessed. Which is why I took the job here. At Night Court. I have a little tiny, teensy bad-boy obsession. And seeing the hot tattooed gang-banger vampires day in and day out, even if they're in cuffs (okay— I *like* them in the cuffs), just does something for me. It lets me live out a fantasy that can never ever be real. Because…

I'm distracted as the hot new felony investigations supervisor walks by. He's in a crisp blue suit and damn! That ass. He turns and I see his face.

My jaw drops. Then so does the rest of my body. I'm crouched by JR's desk, pawing at her legs. "Move. Move! Let me in there." I shove her legs aside and crawl under her desk, bumping my head in the process.

"What?" JR's shock wears off as she bends to stare at me. "What are you doing?"

"Don't! Don't look at me! Sit down! Sit down!"

JR sits. She grimaces and talks like a bad ventriloquist through her teeth. "He's coming this way. What do you want me to do?"

"Get rid of him!" I hide my face, as if that'll just make him go away. Unfortunately, my couple drops of fae blood don't come with cool powers. I can heal quickly, but who can't? What I can't do is make myself disappear. Right now, I'm cursing my ancestors for that.

I hear JR. "Hi," she stands, and I can hear her smooth her skirt, imagine her holding out her hand.

But then, there's a long, awkward silence.

I peek. And see dark green eyes staring at me. Black hair. A five o'clock shadow on a chiseled jaw. The new felony investigation supervisor has squatted down to see me hiding under my best friend's desk. He's smiling. I'm not.

Did I forget to mention, he's my ex?

"Hi Bennett," I try to brazen it out.

"Hello, Lyon," he says softly, trying hard not to laugh.

I bristle. I hate being laughed at. Unless I'm making a joke. So, I decide I need to make one. "Haven't they shown you where we put the confidential files?"

"Under the desk?" He arches an eyebrow but plays along. "No, they skipped that in training."

"Government employees." I roll my eyes. "Always skimping on something."

"Well. Are you done filing?" He bites his lip. And I want to smack him. Half because I used to bite that lip. And the damn memories it brings up make me kind of want to now.

"I guess."

He offers a hand, which I refuse. "Feminist." I offer as an excuse. But, really, I just don't think I can handle touching his skin. Dragons run hot. And his hard, hot hands used to be my personal plaything. I shove back the memories and crawl out, realizing my suit is now a fur-covered nightmare. My pants look like hairy chaps. God, could this get any worse?

JR, always to the rescue (unless it comes to helping me hide under desks), hands me a lint roller. I take it, but I glare at her for the earlier betrayal. She shrugs and mouths, "He's gorgeous."

Bennett sees and grins.

I turn away from both of them and begin frantically rolling my pants. "Darn it." It's useless. Were hair clings like nothing else. And it's scratchy. I sigh and set the lint roller on the desk. Great. With a wave and a "See ya!" I try to walk off.

"Lyon Fox," Bennett calls.

I've always hated how my mom did that to me. Gave me two frickin' animal names.

I try to act like I don't hear Bennett but he just keeps talking. "I'd like to talk. If you have a minute."

I turn around reluctantly. JR is nowhere to be seen. Traitor.

"What?" I tug on a strand of blonde hair and start twisting it around my finger. Then I stop myself. I almost cross my arms, but then I realize that would look defensive. Or draw his attention to my boobs. Would that be better than the look he's giving me right now? I'm still debating when he opens his mouth.

"I don't want things to be weird between us."

Oh no. He didn't go there. Why couldn't he just ignore the awkwardness like a normal person? Why does he want to talk everything out? This was part of why we broke up. This, and a premature declaration of love.

"Weird? What would be weird?" I play dumb, batting my baby blues. "My ex taking a job at my office after he ran off and swore he never wanted to see me again? Why would that be weird?" I decide to do the boob thing. It's a little bitchy to distract him like that. But you know, he started it.

The boobs have their intended effect. His eyes dart down and his retort is derailed for a second.

I smirk, about to turn and walk away again when his voice cuts through me. "That's not how it went down and you know it. I didn't take this job to spite you. I got tired of corporate security. The politics."

"Well, that makes sense. Corporate red tape sucks. Come on over to government. We're way more efficient."

7

"I'm trying to have a serious conversation. I want you to know—"

"Look. I don't want to have this conversation. You do your work. I'll do mine. I will probably never even see you. I work misdemeanors. Not homicides. So, don't worry about me. I won't be a problem for you."

"You're hiding under desks."

"I was filing." I grit my teeth.

He's tentative. He takes a breath before spitting out the next suggestion. I can tell it's hard for him. He's never been a confrontational guy. He's gonna die in felonies. "Maybe we should have coffee. Clear the air. So things won't be so tense."

My eyes widen. He can't be serious. "I'm covered in fur. I have a bruise about to give me a brain bleed from that dang desk. I have to go downstairs. I cannot—no—I will not deal with this, you, right now."

Bennett sucks in a breath and lets it out slowly. "Okay." He sounds disappointed.

This time, he walks away. And while I admire the view, I can't help but feel a little twinge of regret. I stamp it out quickly and run to the ladies' room, where we all have a stash of emergency suits. I can only handle one problem at a time. I need to be at court in five. Being covered in fur balls takes priority.

CHAPTER 2

I hate Arnold. I hate the tacky blue chevron suit I found. The only one in the emergency closet that came close to fitting me. The jacket is so tight I can't button it. The skirt's technically too short for court. And the sleeves have these awesome gold lamé cuffs built in. But it's better than my dog hair monstrosity. So here I stand, cursing bosses, and hairy co-workers, exes who infiltrate your place of work, and bad fashion all at once.

Until the accused are brought out. Suddenly my curses stop. Arnold doesn't seem so bad. He's a nice guy. A great guy. I could kiss him. Maybe. No. Never. But his evil machinations have turned out good for once.

I greet the judge and the public defender. I try not to be obvious as my eyes scan over the pink jumpsuits. (Yeah.

Pink. Someone somewhere thought it'd be a crime deterrent. Don't think that theory panned out.) There are fourteen gorgeous vamps in the holding pen.

DUI is a big problem in Tres Lunas. Only here, the crime's a little different than most places. In a town full of magical creatures, there's not so much driving. Our acronym stands for Drinking (those) Under the Influence. Really, it's an anti-vamp law. Vamps like biting people who are high. Residual effects in the bloodstream or some yadda yadda training I had to sit through. The vamp advocates argue it's a consensual arrangement. The City Council disagrees.

Our nightly arrests would go down by half if they'd just change the law and only arrest those who bite non-consenting humans. But who's gonna listen to a fae who doesn't even have wings? Not my boss. Definitely not the City Council.

The one benefit of our caseload is that I get to see a whole lineup of muscled, dark, misunderstood hotties. Like tonight. I don't know if it was a bachelor party or what, but I can tell immediately the lineup is good.

The third guy down the line winks at me. I try not to react, though I'm sure he can hear my pulse pick up. I scan the rest of the line, eyes bouncing over the two female defendants. Until I see him.

I feel weak, jello-kneed adoration sweep over me. This vamp is a Viking. Blonde hair to his shoulders. Bright blue eyes.

Bulging arms sleeved in tattoos. And my kryptonite. Dimples. Smiling right at me.

That is one hot vamp. I inhale sharply, jealous of whoever he bit. I have to talk myself out of throwing twenty extra charges on him just so he'll be locked up in the dungeon for the next ten years. Having him chained and at my mercy is so tempting...

Damn. I need a date.

I swing my gaze back to Judge Ruddy. He shakes his head, flaming red hair waving back and forth, nose ring glinting. I give him a "So sue me, they're hot!" shrug back and set my case files on the table in front of me.

As courtrooms go, this one's not bad. Black marble. Tall and intimidating ceiling. The bench is about twelve feet high. So even trolls have to crane their necks up to see the judge. Good intimidation factor. But the kicker is the base of the judge's bench. There's a crack at the bottom where neon lights give a fire and brimstone feel. Like the judge has the power to open the gates of hell. It woulda scared the crap outta me as a kid.

Ruddy's Irish lilt rings out over the courtroom, bringing it into session. "Good evenin' ya miscreants. We're here to read tha charges against ya. Then we'll be settin' a date for your pretty faces to come back an' tell me a truth or a lie."

He reads off the docket of names but I don't get to hear Hot

Vamp's name because Shelia, an overeager defense attorney, comes up and starts whispering in my ear.

"Heard you got fresh blood in felonies."

I grimace, not wanting the reminder about Bennett. I change the subject and whisper back. "Are you going to Saffron's campaign meeting?"

Shelia smacks her hair wrap and nods. "Yeah, right after my hair appointment." She's a gorgon, so her hair is an endless source of frustration for her. "I need another round of sedatives for these suckers. You wouldn't believe the tangles when they get wild." She tucks an escaped snake back into her wrap and then looks up at Ruddy.

Shit. He's done with the roll call. Which means we need to get these clowns arraigned so we can all get back to real work. Ruddy starts rattling off dates on the calendar, and I have to pay close attention because sometimes his accent is hard to follow. How a leprechaun ever got elected is beyond me. He's smart as shit. But he's got a mouth full of the mumbles.

We get dates for status conferences set, and those lucky vamps who have the gold to bond out toss it in Ruddy's pot. *Clang. Clang-clang-clang.* Unfortunately, Hot Vamp is one of those with gold. So I won't get to visit my friends down at the dungeon tonight for donuts and a long hard session of staring.

Oh geez. What's wrong with me? I'm borderline pathetic. Okay. Okay. More than borderline. Maybe a toe over.

The vamps file out and I turn to leave but Ruddy stops me. "We've got one more Ms. Foxy."

I grit my teeth and smile. That wasn't a slip of the tongue. But I don't want to tick off the judge. Not yet, anyway. Wait 'til it's worth it.

I wait next to Sheila as the bailiff brings up the next prisoner from the dungeon. I'm expecting some kind of big bad. A troll who smashed up a gnome hill or something. But what I get isn't what I expect. Jerry, the bailiff, escorts a tiny seventy-year-old woman into the courtroom. She has pin-curls like a fifties prima donna and coke bottle thick glasses.

"Your Honor. Is this a joke?"

"Nah. Tisn't. Didna' wanna give the others ideas. So, we left this for last. It's a bit of shame that is." He turns to the defendant. "Tabitha Blue, ye stand accused of Shifting Voyeurism. Ye canna watch the fellas as they shift, even be it through a crystal ball miles away. It's illegal, lass. An' I think you know it, being as this is your fourth offense."

My jaw drops. This little old lady? She's spying on shape shifters?

I mean, I come across a lot of crazy stuff as a paralegal. Like, it's illegal for a gorgon like Sheila to do her own hair. A witch wearing her boots to bed is charged with a 9.301.

13

Making an ugly face at a troll is a violation of penal code 7.91 Instigating Violence.

But this is the first time I've seen someone in for getting off on watching shifters change. I wonder if she likes to watch them turn into humans or turn into animals?

As my mind wanders, old Tabby Blue tries to pull an innocent act on the judge. She blubbers like she's confused. Ruddy sighs. I don't know if he's fooled or sympathetic. But we get a date set for status conference. And Tabby creeps toward him with a shaking hand to put some gold in his pot.

"I was gonna get kibble with this but I guess I can—"

He stalls her hand and sighs. "Go on now, Ms. Blue. I'll release ye on yer own recognizance. Get home. Anni' don' wanna be hearing no more of you spyin' on the fellas. Alright?"

"Yes, Your Honor," her voice trembles just the right amount.

I am in awe. I'm in the presence of a master. Tabby flashes me a grin as she walks out of the courtroom, pocketing her gold. I want to be her so bad it hurts.

I turn back to Ruddy, who's packing up.

"Your Honor. I think you just got punked."

Sheila stifles a giggle and hurries out as Ruddy glares down at me from the bench.

"Approach, lil miss know-it-all."

Man. I was just supposed to cover for Bella. Now I'm in trouble with Ruddy. Which means trouble with Arnold. Which means an even longer night in this stupid suit.

"Your Honor, I'm sorry. I wasn't thinking—" I near the brimstone. It is, in fact, quite intimidating. The neon messes with your eyes as you tilt your head back, back, back. My neck cracks.

Ruddy gives me the stink eye. "That much is clear. Ye speak to me like that again, lass, an' you'll be in contempt."

"Yes, Your Honor. Sorry, Your Honor."

I leave the courtroom as quickly as possible. I smack myself as I enter the elevator. "Snap out of it. Shut your mouth, you big dope. Who does that?"

Of course, who should walk up behind me at that very moment? Someone with heavy footfalls and expensive shoes. Gah! Does the embarrassment never end? I seriously consider just staring at the walls of the elevator for the entire ride. But I pull up my big girl pants and turn around.

Immediately, I wish I hadn't.

"Bennett." I try to fake a smile, but my lips just manage a hard line. What was he doing down at the misdemeanor court? Was he following me? Monitoring me? Watching me eff up?

My cheeks flame.

"I don't think you've been that red since our first date—"

"No." I cut him off. He did not just go there. He did not just remind me about that little Indian restaurant, where they flipping lock the bathrooms like it's a truck stop.

After nine months of tagging along on the outskirts of his group of friends, crushing hard on him, he'd finally asked me out. And I was nervous. I had to pee.

It's not my fault I didn't realize you had to ask for a key. There were damn cloth napkins on the tables! I stood there for almost ten minutes, like an idiot, thinking someone was in there in front of me. It wasn't 'til some lady walked up with a key that I even knew. Bennett had asked for the check by the time I got back. He thought I'd ditched him. Was ready to hate my guts.

Then he thought ... I don't even want to think about what he thought about my guts after that. Probably that I had IBS or something. Needless to say, there was no first date kiss. There almost was no second date. And I came so close to losing my witty bantering, heart thumping, giggle extracting, sweaty palm inducing sweetheart ... I had a panic attack after that first date.

My palms are sweaty now. Why is he here? Why is he always here when I embarrass myself? Why did he take a job at my office? It's torture.

I feel Ben's green gaze on me. I cannot look. It's like fire. I wish I could just dissolve.

I scooch over to the corner. Distance. Need distance. The doors start to close. A hand stops them.

I want to thank the savior that rescued me from a six-story elevator ride from hell. But when the doors open all the way, my jaw goes slack. Hot Vamp walks on, pink jumpsuit gone, fully tailored black shirt and slacks replacing it.

Immediately the tension ratchets up. At first, I think it's just because I'm about to internally combust from some potent combo of lust and embarrassment. But then I realize the guys are glaring daggers at each other.

"Mr. French," Hot Vamp inclines his head at Bennett and comes to stand by me along the side wall. Close. Too close. We could almost touch. If his arm moved just a little…

Shit. I start to panic. A cold sweat forms on my spine. My heart races.

Hot Vamp turns toward me and smiles. "Hey, gorgeous. Didn't catch your name in there." He starts to extend a hand.

I stumble into Bennett, my mind in full on panic mode. "Germaphobe. Conflict of interest. Um… Lesbian!"

Hot Vamp laughs. "The lady doth protest too much, I think."

Bennett puts his hands on my shoulders. Supposedly he's being reassuring, but I shrug him off, unable to do this. I hit the emergency stop button. I push at the doors. Like an idiot. Like a caged animal. "Out. I need to get out."

"It's okay Ly," Bennett tries to calm me down.

But I'm in flight mode. I scratch at the doors like a mad woman. "Out."

Hot Vamp leans over behind us, undoes the emergency button, and pushes the button for the next floor. The ding signals my release, and I stumble out of the elevator. I head straight for the woman's restroom and pull out my cell. I dial JR. "Come help me."

"Honey, what's wrong?" She immediately shifts into momma bird mode when she hears my voice. "I'll take them out, whoever they are."

It takes a minute before I can calm down enough to tell her. "There was a vamp. In the elevator. We almost touched."

I hear her intake of breath. "Oh my stars. Where are you?"

"Bathroom. Second floor. I think."

"Don't move. I'm coming."

CHAPTER 3

J R is there, petting my hair and rocking me back and forth.

"He's not Alec, honey. He's not."

"I ... I know." I sniffle. Even the dark Viking god can't measure up to my old high school boyfriend. A gorgeous vamp with blond curls who looked like a cherub all grown up and naughtified. His grin. I doubt I'll ever get over him. My first love, my first everything. He ruined me for vamps. I might be drawn to them. But I will never ever touch one again. It's a toxic combo.

"I'm sorry. I think I'm being over-dramatic. But having Bennett in the elevator was painful, and then this vamp. Like, I haven't been that drawn to anyone in a long time."

"Wait. Back up. Painful?"

"Bennet is *that* ex. The one who ran away."

"Honey," JR rubs my back sympathetically. "If I'd known he was *that* guy, I'd never have left you alone with him at my desk. I'm sorry."

I shrug. "I'm over it. I have to be over it." I rub a hand over my face, trying to pull myself together.

JR notices I'm coming back to life and she spurs the process by asking, "What do you think that stain over there is?"

That's all the prompting I need to get up off the bathroom floor.

She helps me clean up and I return to work, using my hair as a protective shield, vowing never, ever to get it bobbed.

I ignore Arnold's waddling, especially after he half-shifts into wolf form (the lower half only) around midnight. I hate when he does that. I've complained to HR; they don't do a damn thing. I think he does it just because he wants to walk around the office without pants.

I finish work about an hour before dawn, utterly exhausted. I shut down my four-year-old, slower than a snail computer and wave goodbye to Alexander—our receptionist and the resident man-whore of the office. JR has already left.

I stumble outside alone and call a Broomer using the

Broomer app on my cell. Two minutes later, I'm on a broom behind a witch, headed for home. I want nothing more than to hop in the shower and crawl into bed, but I promised Saffron.

I curse myself for volunteering to help with her campaign, though really I couldn't just have stood by and watched my mentor go-it-alone. Saffron's a judge running for a City Council member spot. She's the judge that used to take me aside and ream my butt for being rude in court. She'll be ticked if she learns about today. I'm hoping Ruddy is as forgiving to stand-in paralegal prosecutors as he is to little old ladies.

I fish through my purse for my keys. I don't feel them.

"Gah, this the is best day ever! My keys are never where they're supposed to be."

I end up dumping out my entire purse and kneeling on the stoop to sort through my trash. I live on the second floor of a four-plex built in the sixties. It's outdated, but close to work. It's got built-in shelves that I've filled to overflowing and a perfect balcony that faces the dawn. The world's best reading spot. Those were its selling features. Not the elderly neighbors. The dog-shifter downstairs who barks incessantly. Or the curry smell from Mrs. Snow's apartment; the woman deludes herself into believing she's a witch doctor and mixes together potions that smell worse than rat poison. But hey, it's home. It's mine. And now I can't get inside and I'm digging on my stoop like a lunatic through a pile of useless receipts. That's how Jacob finds me.

"Um, ride's here." Jacob Watts is Saffron's husband, and my stand-in for a father. He's a sixty-three-year old coyote shifter and one of the best people in the entire world. That's a fact. I pop up to give him a hug.

His brown eyes sparkle with mischief. "What's going on?"

"You know what's going on." I grumble and hold out a hand. He chuckles. I am a constant loser of things. It's an annoying habit, one I can't seem to kick no matter how many post-its I stick on my own shirt. The three neighbors have keys. JR has one, and Jacob and Saffron each do as well. I sigh as I unlock my door and push it open. At least Jacob's hardware store keeps me well-stocked with new locks and keys.

"Five minutes. I promise. I just have to change."

"What? Blue's your color." Jacob is a joker. He thinks he's hilarious. I roll my eyes.

"Can't be competing with your wife at her own campaign meeting now can I?"

He gives a shrug.

I push him on the shoulder. "Hey, you should be excited. You're about to be famous. The arm candy of a City Councilor."

"Yeah. Yeah."

"You don't seem excited."

He sighs and sits on my second-hand purple velvet couch.

"I want her to be happy." Jacob's not big on limelight. Saffron, being a judge, has always lived in it. Opposites attract I guess.

Jacob fingers a dead plant on the coffee table as I head for the bedroom. "What was this?"

"No clue," I yell as I kick the door shut. JR's magic includes growing plants. And she's constantly giving them to me. Obviously, I'm a great caretaker. Thank goodness her powers do not involve small animals.

I rip off the wretched blue suit and throw on yoga pants and a light sweater. I run a comb through my stick straight hair and find some lingering were-hair from the floor. Great. I check myself in the mirror to make sure there isn't more. Overall, I look like a human. Like my dad. Semi-attractive, blonde hair and blue eyes. Except for the bright blue jewel embedded in my chin and my black toenails, you'd never know I have some garbled mix of pixie and fae-blood. I grab some snack pack cupcakes and a bag of jelly beans out of the cabinet (improv dinner) and tell Jacob I'm ready to go.

He goes into the bathroom to shift while I grab my saddle from its hook on the wall and toss it over my shoulder. Jacob trots out, his grey coat sleek as he noses me to hurry up. I toss his clothes into a bag for him and we head out.

Riding a coyote is not the most comfortable way to get around town, but it's pretty efficient. Especially when you eat a shrink pill before the run.

I eat the spelled tablet I keep on-hand for Jacob's rides. Two seconds later, I'm a pint-size pipsqueak; I'm about two feet tall so I fit perfectly in the saddle on Jacob's back.

As he runs, I wish I'd brought a jacket, because the chill of fall nips at my skin. We're in So. Cal, but the coastal winds get me. I am generally not one of those bikini-on-the-beach types. I prefer jeans and a jacket at pretty much all times, thank you.

Jacob jumps into a pile of dead leaves. And that's what starts the game. I yell, "Yee haw!" and suddenly he's a bucking bronco. This is a small part of why he's my favorite person on the planet after JR. He knows what fun is and isn't too embarrassed to have it.

We play until we get close to the parking lot of the casino. Too many humans from out of town could see. Technically, the town is spelled. Humans can't get into most parts. The casino has exceptions. Enchantments and drunkenness work in tandem to keep magic under wraps.

Obvi, if we go to human cities, the restrictions get worse. But Tres Lunas has spelled boundaries. So, the second humans step out of town, they forget what they saw here. In that way, Tres is kinda like Vegas. If they see it here, they forget it here.

I slide off Jacob's back, grab the saddle, and we walk toward the side doors of the palatial Abra Casino.

As we round a corner, I see construction. The whole backside of the building is blown out. And it hasn't been cleaned up yet.

Matthew Boolye is the cajun real estate mogul who owns Abra Casino. He's ponying up most of the money for Saffron's campaign. I think he's hoping to time her win with the opening of a new theater for the casino. Free press or something. But whatever. I'm happy Saffron found a sugar daddy donor, and I don't have to go collecting door-to-door.

Jacob darts into a changing room set just inside the door for shifters. I toss the bag of clothes in after him and pull the door shut (which is no small feat considering I'm still only about two feet tall). While he shifts and changes, I grab a second spelled tablet to return me to normal size. I spend a second wishing they had spelled tablets for boobs. I mean, mine are good. But I kinda think every woman wonders … But no one's been able to isolate the spell enough for body parts. Shame.

When Jacob steps out we tromp down a hall lit by floating fairy lights into the meeting room. Sheila Stone is already there.

Saffron and Matthew walk in laughing a second later. I'm glad to see her laughing. She's typically such a workaholic, I don't see her relax. Jacob and I joke that she sleeps in her courtroom. We bought her a quilt with gavels on it last Christmas so she could keep it at the office. (Surprisingly, she was not as amused as we were.)

Sheila calls the meeting to order. She's technically the organizer of the whole campaign shindig. Which—thank goodness. Because my ideas about running a campaign are limited.

My great contribution so far has been the cheesy slogan: Vote Saffron to Spice up City Council. And that little piece of brilliance only came after three glasses of wine.

Sheila pulls out a list and pops on a pair of cat-eye reading glasses. "All right, the were-bears want to have a hug-a-thon fundraiser, which is basically an excuse for them to semi-gamble on who can squeeze the other until they pass out. But it did bring in a lot of money for Ruddy's campaign for judge, so I think we need to consider it."

Saffron nods as she pulls her waist length brown hair into a loose ponytail over her shoulder. She's the granddaughter of a thunderbird, so her hair is intertwined with a mix of feathers. Very unruly. (I think she and Sheila initially bonded over hair care.) "I'm not crazy about the hug-a-thon thing, but I'll sleep on it."

Matthew interjects, "We could have it in front of my new

condo property. It has a large lawn. So long as they don't get too unruly ..."

Sheila adds a note to her list. "Got it. Could work, but I do want to point out if we have so many fund-raising activities on your rental properties, you might isolate people who are going to vote for Georgina."

Matthew puffs up his chest and shrugs. "Don't want to rent to imbeciles anyway."

I don't like his comment.

I don't like Matthew, to be honest. He's one of those older guys that's always just struck me as creepy. Can't quite put my finger on why. It's not the lizard scales on his skin. I'm not judgmental like that. It's not the weight. He has a paunch but he's over fifty.

Maybe it's those stupid paisley bow ties he wears. No. Not it. Maybe it's his arrogance. Though I can find that attractive in some guys. I think there's a slime to his Alpha vibe. If that makes sense.

I shelve my negative thoughts. Not the time for them. Tonight we're going to discuss Saffron's upcoming debate against Georgina Knight, her vamp opponent.

Sheila pulls out a new piece of paper. "Okay, so I have some of the questions we can go over. I would just start with a brainstorm—"

The door smacks open, interrupting Sheila mid-sentence. In strides a willowy blonde in a white sheathe dress. A human might think she's a model. But they'd be wrong. She's all vamp. Part of the most prominent vamp family in town.

Georgina Knight has interrupted our meeting.

"Well, isn't this a cozy location to plot your smear campaign."

Saffron smooths her broom skirt and stands, all polite when her opponent just rammed open the door and hurled an accusation. Me? I just wanna punch the bitch. How dare she?

"Hello, Ms. Knight. We were about to review some debate topics. Is there something I can help you with?"

"Yes. Call the news and let them know whatever crap you fed them was a lie."

Saffron's eyebrows shoot up. "I'm sorry. I haven't spoken with any reporters about you." Her eyes circle the room. Everyone shrugs.

"Apparently no one here knows what you're referring to, Ms. Knight." I love that tone Saffron uses when she puts people in their place. Gah. She's kind of my hero.

You can practically see the steam building up behind Georgina's ears. Her pale cheeks turn pink. "You're a liar. You lied to Channel Thirteen. You lied to your husband. You're lying to me now!" Her voice builds to a screech.

Matthew's at her side quickly. "I'll thank you to leave my property at once."

Georgina mimics him. "I'll thank you to stick to your contracts at once. How about that? You think I'm going to—" Matthew and Jacob go to grab her by the elbows, but she's across the room in an instant. Vamp super-speed beats shifter strength. She turns burning eyes back to Saffron.

"You had better make sure that piece doesn't air tomorrow. Or I will expose every filthy secret you have. And I will destroy you." She waves her hands in big sweeping gestures. I think it's meant to be threatening. But honestly? She looks ridiculous. She needs to practice her threats in a mirror or something.

"What piece? What story?"

Georgina's in Saffron's face the next second. "I have never drained a human."

Saffron's face pales. "I would never accuse—"

Georgina's hand smacks her. And then the crazed woman is across the room again. She's lucky she's so fast. Jacob—who's shifted—would have her neck otherwise. He stands guard over Saffron.

Is this some kind of ploy? I watch Georgina's hands. Is she here to plant a bug? Put a tongue-tying spell on Saffron before the debate? As if Saffron would ever accuse someone of simultaneous murder and violation of magical secrecy. This has got to be a ruse.

I clap, drawing everyone's eyes. "Ha-ha. Very dramatic. If you've put a single spell on Saffron or anyone here, that will be a violation of campaign ethics, you know."

Smack. Georgina's grabbing my arm. "You—" She grabs me by the throat. "You little piece of garbage. You little slut. I didn't know you were still in town. Didn't know you were still alive."

Matthew's called security. They finally arrive. A burly troll grabs Georgina around the waist and forcefully hauls her off me.

Jacob's at my side, checking my neck. "Are you okay?" His coyote voice is a bit high-pitched.

That freaking hurt! But, not wanting to cause drama, I wave off his concern. "The bruises should be gone in a couple of hours." The one minuscule power from my fae family. I usually mock my quick healing, since I've never even broken a bone. But right now, I'm thankful. Without it, I'd be keeled over begging Jacob to take me to a witch doctor this instant.

I look around to check on everyone else.

Matthew has Saffron's elbow, checking to see if she's calmed down. Sheila is taking notes rapid-fire in her notebook. She's the only one that seems completely unaffected.

"Well," Sheila slams her notebook shut. "That was interesting."

It's not so easy for me to shake off Georgina's attack. Especially with Jacob eying me with fatherly concern. I grab my bag of jellybeans and tell the group, "I need a breather. I'll be outside."

CHAPTER 4

I go into the hall, and deliberately walk away from the beckoning fairy lights and the machine gunfire ping-ping-ping of the slots. I turn toward the construction plastic. I do *not* want to encounter Georgina again.

Luckily there's a slit in the plastic so I can escape to the rubble pile outside. It's nearing dawn. Watching the fading stars helps me calm down. I walk away from the casino through the rubble, thinking.

I've seen Georgina a couple times over the years. She's either glossed over me in the crowd or literally not seen me. Yeah, she's self-absorbed like that. She's never attacked me. Never even acted like me dating her brother ten million years ago was a big deal. She must really be unhinged if little things like that are setting her off.

I pop open the bag of jellybeans and plop down onto a broken slab on concrete. I contemplate what the stress of an election can do to a person. I hope Saffron doesn't go mental like that. Or I'll have to rescue Jacob and hide him in my spare room, under my massive stacks of trashy paperbacks.

A handful of sugar. That's what I need. I crunch the shells and let the jellybean goodness coat my tongue. I try to find my mental happy place. Which somehow must include men with bulging muscles, because I turn my head and see Hot Vamp—the guy from the courthouse. Great. I probably have concrete dust all over my butt. Don't stand.

"Hey, beautiful." Those dimples tempt me. But I haven't checked my teeth for jellybeans yet, so no way I'm smiling. Tight lipped grin only.

"What are you doing here?" I ask.

"Stalking." He winks. "Just kidding. Can I sit?"

I shrug, my mind not really processing his words. He's lost the tailored shirt and a very tight t-shirt is clinging to sculpted pecs. Oh, hotness drizzled in honey, I'm in trouble.

Hot Vamp sits on a concrete slab about three feet away. Okay. My irrational vamp-panic meter can deal with that. It's not too close.

What is it about this guy? Yeah, I like drooling. But he takes temptation to a new level. I hold out the bag of jellybeans, part friendly gesture, part to put a barrier between us so I don't yield to temptation and ruin years of hard-fought self-control. "Jellybean?"

"No thanks." He holds out his hand to shake. "I'm Luke."

I hold up sticky fingers with jellybean stains. "Can't." What I don't say is that I won't touch him, ever. Because I would not be able to control myself. Which means he wouldn't be able to control himself. Which means ...

"Well, can I get a name at least?"

"Lyon."

"No. You're lying."

I roll my eyes. "Original. So original."

He laughs. It's a low growly sexy sound. "Couldn't help it."

Now I can't help it. I laugh too. I can't believe it. I'm actually interacting on a semi-normal, non-gawker, non-freakout level with a vamp. Way to go me!

"So, don't you need to go find a hole to hide in or something?" I flick a wrist at the sky. "Moon's about to set."

He sighs. "Yeah. That's why I came here actually. Thought I might find some peace and quiet."

"At a construction site? At a casino?" My eyes narrow. He was totally here for the burlesque show.

Luke shrugs, the picture of innocence. "Cleanup crew is working another job. Won't be here for a day or two."

"How do you know...? Oh, you work construction." That explains the brawn. I try very hard to maintain eye contact. Not to picture him sweaty and dirty, ripping his t-shirt off to wipe his brow. Enough! I need a frickin' date. That's it. I'm asking out Alexander the receptionist. Tomorrow.

"I actually work in management. But I really like the little blush you have going, picturing me in construction. So, we'll just leave that image be."

I choke on a jellybean.

Luke stands to help, and I wave him off with wild arms.

"No! No touching."

"Okay," He stays standing though, until it's clear I'm not gonna die.

"Do you mind if I ask... about what happened on the elevator?"

I sigh. "I can't talk about that." I stuff in some more jellybeans to prevent myself from spilling the beans to a hot stranger.

"Okay. But, I just really need to clarify one point. You're not a lesbian?"

That sets me off. I laugh so hard I choke again. And this time, I'm really choking.

36

I smack my own chest. It does nothing. I can't … can't—

Luke's suddenly behind me, arms around my torso, Heimlich in process.

Though I can't breathe, my brain still manages to think (in its oxygen deprived state) 'No. Get away. I don't want to hurt you.'

Jellybeans go flying out of my mouth. And my internal freak out suddenly becomes very verbal. "Get back! I don't want to hurt—"

Slam.

I fall into the rubble, ripping my yoga pants and skinning my knee.

A roar fills my ears. I look around. Luke's disappeared. A gust of air presses me down into sharp bits of plaster.

I look up. There, in the sky, is a dragon. It has Luke in its claws.

Another beat of wings stronger than helicopter blades and I'm curled up in a ball on the rubble. Something sharp scratches at my side.

The dragon turns, intending to fly south, and I recognize the red-black pattern of its scales. No effing way.

I stand. "Bennett!" I shriek. "What the hell are you doing?"

Bennett drops Luke—who would have died if he'd been

human. But, being vamp, he just starts running mid-air. He creates enough of a jet stream to control his landing. And then he's off, a blur heading toward the wooded mountains on the outskirts of Tres Lunas.

Bennett looks at me. Then at the trail of dust Luke's kicked up.

"Don't you dare!" I scream.

He snorts, a cloud of smoke billowing from his nostrils. It immediately makes the entire place smell like a campground. Does he listen?

He does not. My blood boils.

He streaks through the sky like a maniac after a perfectly innocent vampire who was just trying to stop me from choking to death. On a jellybean.

Bennett's following me. He's crazy. Thoughts of restraining orders fill my head.

But then I turn. My budding rant is cut off. Because across the pile of rubble, I see Georgina Knight.

Her jaw drops. Suddenly, my head spikes with pain. I see red sparks. And fade to black.

CHAPTER 5

I wake up in the dark. I'm disoriented. Last thing I remember, I was outside, and it was almost dawn.

Now, I'm in a stone room, with a packed dirt floor. No window. I sit up slowly. My head is pounding like I just fought a troll. I carefully turn my neck. I'm pretty sure my head's about to fall off and just roll down into my lap. Seriously. It hurts that bad. But I forget the pain when I see bars.

OMG.

I'm in a cell. I've been kidnapped. Holy mother of goats. I am in some mad Frankenstein's basement and he's gonna—

My monumental freak out stops when I see JR step up to the bars.

"Hey honey," she says softly from the other side.

That is not the right tone for a joke. I don't think. My head's still unsteady. I touch the back. It hurts. Is that dried blood?

"Where—"

"You're in the dungeon."

Jail! I'm in jail!

"What?"

"Do you remember what happened last night?"

I close one eye to stop the room from spinning. "I covered for Bella. Got off work late. Went to Saffron's meeting."

She nods, encouraging me. "And then?"

"I don't know." The memories are hazy. "I went outside. Hot Vamp was there. Then Bennett … I passed out?" I end with a question, because I really don't know what happened.

"Hey!" Golem X's voice booms from down the hall. "You're allowed to bring her that stuff. You didn't say nothing about talking to her."

"Sorry!" JR holds up a hand, placating the golem who oversees the dungeon. Golems are un-bribe-able. Apparently being made out of mud and brought to life by spells renders you immune to pleading. Emotion. Decency. Makes them great guards. Until you're stuck in jail for unknown reasons and they don't want to let your best friend talk to you. I glare at Golem X. He's unimpressed.

JR hands a narrow bag through the bars. "I brought you some stuff. A couple pillows, a blanket. Your camera. I thought it might help pass the time. They had the witch scan it all for spells on the way in. Your jellybeans were confiscated. Yum tax, they said. Sorry."

I take the bag. "Is this real? Like real real?"

She sighs. "Unfortunately, hon."

"What happened?"

She opens her mouth but glances sideways. Golem X must be watching. "I'll be back soon." Tears fill her eyes before she walks away. And that makes me very, very scared.

Why am I in here? What's JR afraid of?

I'M WAITING FOR HOURS IN THE DARK CELL. FEAR SLOWLY fades to impatience as I wait for someone to freakin' tell me something.

I stop guessing why I'm here after about hour four. They'll tell me. I'll make them. When someone finally shows up. Why haven't they shown up?

I try to get comfortable on my pillows. Can't. Try to bunch up the rainbow quilt JR brought me so I have a seat cushion to soften the floor. Doesn't work. It sucks. I alternate between killing my elbows by laying on my stomach and flipping through old photos on my camera and laying on my back and hurting my ass while I stare at the camera settings.

I will never take my old mattress for granted again.

I flick through photos for the eighth time. My hobby—twisted as it is—is taking photos of old crime scenes. I dunno why. Well. I kinda do. The rainbow splatter of ectoplasm after a ghost brawl is gorgeous. Especially at dawn. Ever seen a closeup of the fungi that grows on troll's teeth? You can get a great shot if you find one in the field where illegal fights went down. These tiny pink flower fungi grow in the spaces between their teeth. It's crazy cool. In a weird way, I admit. But still. I love discovering details like that. Things other people don't see.

I know. I'm a freak. But I have to break up the monotony of vamp-ogling sometimes.

I flick back to a charred building that housed a witch before her spell went wrong. Not my best work. But still.

"You should have used infrared," a voice near my ear whispers.

I drop my camera.

A thin, scaly grey hand picks it up and hands it back to me. Its owner is a three-foot-tall fire salamander.

"Who are you?" I breathe.

"Noah." My cellmate replies with a grin. His name is very human for a salamander. Generally his kind take a lotta joy in making us try and pronounce things like "Snnnishlsessssl."

"Hi, Noah. I'm Ly-ly." I opt for friendly. "How'd you get in here?"

"I've been in here."

"Oh." I don't know what to say. I mean, how self-absorbed am I not to have noticed my cellmate?

"I've been on the ceiling."

That makes me feel a little better.

"You should have taken that picture with infrared," Noah gestures back toward my camera. "Witch runes show up awesome on infrared. They glow."

"Oh. Good tip. Never tried that. You shoot?"

"Used to."

"I bet you could get amazing angles climbing up on the ceilings."

"Yeah, until I fell off one too many times."

"Didn't think about that."

"Gets hard on the hips after awhile."

I offer Noah one of my pillows. He curls up on it and lets out a satisfied sigh. "Thanks."

"So, whatcha' in for?" I sit back against the wall.

"Arson."

I nod. Not surprising for a fire salamander.

"You?" he asks.

I shrug. "Dunno."

Footfalls interrupt our conversation. Noah cocks his head to listen. "Well, I think you're about to find out."

Who do I least want to see in the world right now? Hint: Arnold's a close second.

Bennett brings the keys to my cell.

"Fox. Come on. We need to talk."

I jump to my feet.

"What's going on? What am I doing here? Why are you stalking me? What happened? How long have I been in there? When are you letting me go? I didn't do anything!"

Words tumble out as I follow on his toes. He ignores me and it makes me feel like a yappy puppy. Which does not make me happy.

We ride the elevator in silence, and I'm suddenly aware of how bad I smell. I'm still in my ripped clothes from last night.

Bennett ushers me down a hallway, into a room I don't recognize until I'm seated. Then I see the two-way glass. Shit. I'm in an interrogation room.

"Tell me about what happened last night."

"You tell me why I'm here."

Bennett just stares.

"I dunno. I stroked out or something. Woke up here."

"Did you see the victim at all?"

"Victim? What victim?"

My heart rate picks up. I mean, I know I was tossed in jail. But for what? Best I could come up with was trespassing or violating some kind of construction safety code. What do they think I did?

"Georgina Knight was murdered."

I stand, knocking my chair back. It falls to the floor with a dull thunk. "What?!"

The memories flood back. I saw her. My head hurt like a mother. That's it. Shit. They think I killed her?

"I got knocked out." My hand reaches toward the back of my head. Yeah, that's got to be dried blood.

Bennett stands and rights my chair for me. He helps ease me back into it. Normally, I'd protest, but right now I'm so in shock. I can't even …

"Why don't you back up a bit. We got statements from others that you were at Saffron Watts' campaign meeting."

I give him the play by play of the night after he returns to his seat. When I get to choking on a jellybean, Bennett rubs a hand over his face and groans.

"That's what happened? Why did you freak out if he was saving you?"

"Because I don't let vampires touch me," I snap.

"Damnit. I thought he was attacking you."

"Why were you following me anyway?"

"I wasn't."

Oh, that pisses me off. First, he shows up *my* work. Then he follows me around like a crazy person. Now, he's locked me up and is accusing me of murder?

"Yes. You are exhibiting stalker-like tendencies. You got a job at my office. Followed me down to a misdemeanor courtroom. Followed me to that campaign meeting. Then locked me up. *You* are acting way more like a murderer than I am."

That pisses Bennett off. He leans forward and bares his teeth. "I wasn't following *you*, idiot. I was following Luke Hawkins."

My jaw drops. "Why?"

Bennett shakes his head and drops back into his seat. "You need to finish telling me about your night."

"You need to prove you're not a stalker and that you have some kind of grounds for this arrest."

"You were the last person to see Georgina Knight alive."

"So? I was the last person to see my grandma alive, too. Doesn't make me a murderer."

"Eighty-five percent of murderers are found next to the body."

"Eighty-five percent of murders are committed by trolls," I shoot back.

Bennett sighs. "I'm gonna get coffee. You want coffee?"

This sounds like a peace offering. Or maybe he's giving me a minute to cool off because I'm worked up. I mean, me, a murderer? The thought makes me see red. Whew. I do need to calm down. Murderers get defensive, right? I shouldn't get offended. It will make me look defensive. And I didn't do anything.

"Coffee's great. Thanks."

"Four sugars and milk?"

He remembers how I take my coffee? We haven't gone out for like two years. Any other day, I might be impressed. Today, I just wave him away.

Arnold slips into the interrogation room while Bennett's getting coffee. He's wearing pants at least. But he's also wearing a shit-eating grin. "It's my sad duty to inform you that you'll be put on administrative leave for the duration of this investigation."

My heart sinks. Another little piece of poo to add to the shit-storm. No, turd-tornado. No, stool tsunami. My mind has officially entered meltdown. This is real. I, Lyon Fox, have been arrested for murder. And I'm about to lose my job.

Arnold starts to walk out.

"Wait. Is that paid administrative leave?"

Arnold turns back, his grin even wider. "That all depends on the outcome of the investigation."

Awesome.

Bennett returns with coffee as I'm fighting off tears.

"I didn't do this," I state flatly. I recite the rest of my night for him, ending with how I saw Georgina and then felt something split my head in two. Bennett comes around and inspects the back of my head. He sees the crusted blood and uses his phone to start taking pictures.

"I'm gonna part your hair okay?" His fingers dig into what's become a nest of snarls. I don't protest. I let him. Because I want to prove I'm not a murderer.

Bennett's finger traces a line up and down my scalp. "There's a fresh scar here. Healing quickly though. Can you hold your hair apart while I take pictures?"

I comply, pulling my hair tight.

Bennett finishes and taps my head to let me know he's done. "Just a sec. I'll be right back."

He walks out and I'm left wondering if the scar on my head is enough proof to convince the powers that be that I'm just a victim here. Because I am. How could they even think it was me?

Bennett's back in the room in under a minute. "Okay, I sent Bella out to nose around the crime scene. She's gonna look for whatever was used to knock you out."

"You didn't see it last night?"

He shakes his head. "You'd lost a lot of blood. For all we knew, the injury to your head came from the struggle."

"What struggle?"

"The murder."

"Vamps are way stronger and faster than I am. Maybe I could trap a dumb one. But Georgina's not dumb. Wasn't dumb. How the hell am I supposed to have killed her?"

Bennett eyes me uncomfortably. "I'm not at liberty to say just yet."

If there was a struggle, I should have more scars. I stand and start inspecting my body. My right sleeve is crusty. I peel it back. My forearm has a crisscross of jagged white lines. And then I see them. My entire body stiffens. At my wrist, are two tiny little holes. Two puncture wounds.

I look up at Bennett in horror. "Did she bite me?"

I PASS OUT. LITERALLY JUST FALL OVER. I DON'T KNOW HOW long I'm out, Bennett cradling my head like some damn maiden in distress—but it must be awhile. When I come to, Bella's back.

She strides right into the investigation room and up to Bennett, who helps me to my feet and then goes into a corner with her. They whisper discreetly. And by discreetly, I mean like five-year-olds who can't keep a secret.

I'm too dazed to listen. This situation is my worst nightmare come to life.

Bennett walks over to me with a chunk of broken plaster in his hands. Metal mesh protrudes from the end. He holds the mesh next to my right arm. I pull my sleeve back to show the scars on my arm. It's a match.

Bella takes photos while Bennett holds the plaster over my arm, next to it. Holds it up by the scar on the back of my head. Then he sends Bella off with instructions to bag the plaster and develop prints.

"So, does this mean you believe me?"

"It means there's some evidence on your side."

"Way to two-step around that one." I rub a hand over my face and sink into my seat. I don't want to ask my next question. But I have to.

"Bennett ... did she turn human?"

He tenses. Stiff as a board. Yup. And now he's back to thinking I did this. I hate that look in his eyes.

My eyes tear up. "There's a reason I don't let vamps touch me, Ben."

"I'm listening."

My throat starts to close but I force the words out. Tell the truth, dummy. "I dated her brother a long time ago. High school."

Bennett waits like a good interrogator, letting the silence build. Damn him! Don't use your stupid techniques on me! But they work. Words spill out before my brain catches up to my tongue.

"Alec left after he broke up with me. He's never come back."

Bennett writes in his little black notebook. "So that's why she attacked you? Because she blames you for her brother leaving?"

"What?"

"We have witnesses who say she attacked you at the meeting. Did she do it again outside? It's not murder if it self-defense, Ly-ly."

I stand. "No. You don't understand. I'm not the murderer. I'm not a killer. I didn't—"

Bennett stands too. He holds his hands out as if to pacify me.

"I don't need your patronizing. I'm not the murderer, I'm telling you. I'm the damn murder weapon."

Bennett just stares at me blankly.

"When I was fifteen, Alec bit me. And he turned human." Shame washes over me as I relive the horror of that moment.

The passion that lit Alec up in the aftermath of our first time. How he asked if he could bite me. 'Just a sip. To make you even more mine.' I had no idea back then.

"What?"

"My blood turns vamps human. Someone smacked me with that plaster last night. Scraped up my arm. What vamp can resist easy blood? Someone used me to lure Georgina closer. My blood made Georgina human. That would make her an easy mark."

Bennett runs his hands through his hair. "I've never heard of anything like this."

"I know."

"You never told anyone."

I shake my head. "I was fifteen. A kid."

"If he turned human, was his memory wiped?"

The law says someone who loses his or her powers has to be wiped. Because once you're 'humanized,' your alliances change. You're more likely to out your former pack or share your coven's secrets.

I nod, tears starting despite myself. "His family sent him away. Thought a new start would be easier for him, since they were all vamp."

"So, the parents can verify your story."

"Yeah."

"Wouldn't Georgina have known?"

I shrug. "She's older. Didn't live in the house at the time. I dunno."

"So, she might not have known your blood does this?"

"You'd have to talk to her parents."

Bennett sighs. "How many part-fae are in this town?"

"Four? Maybe. Most of them get brought beyond the Veil." This is so not the moment to reflect on my mother's below-average parenting skills.

"This isn't a common vamp-fae reaction?"

I shrug. "I've never heard of it. But I'm a mixed bag. My fae family are kinda liberal in their marriages." This is the phrase my grandmother taught me to use instead of saying my mother and an aunt were tramps.

"Okay. I'll see what I can find out. If anyone else has a record of something like this. Has it ever happened to you again?"

"You mean did I ever intentionally violate Statute 1.38? Theft of Power? No. God. I was horrified. Am horrified. I haven't touched a vamp in nine years." Even though I'm drawn to vamps, I'm their worst nightmare. I know that.

"I just had to ask."

"I know."

Bella comes back in, hauling a practice dummy on her back and box in her hands. She ignores the fact that she interrupted us as she proceeds to take my fingerprints. Bennett lets her, watching me silently. She gets my prints on a card, then she hauls the dummy up onto the table.

"Place your fingers around the neck please."

What? This is not protocol. I raise my eyebrows at her, then look at Bennett. He gives a slight nod.

"Why?"

Bella sighs as though explaining things to me is the biggest inconvenience in the world. "Because we need prints on multiple surfaces. Okay?"

I just covered for her last night. And this is how she's gonna act? I squint and deliberately stick my fingers on the stomach of the practice dummy. "There."

"The neck, not the torso."

"You have prints on multiple surfaces."

Bennett interjects. "Just cooperate, Lyon."

"I've been cooperating. This looks like some kind of bull-spit set up."

"It's not."

"Why do you need it?"

Bella tries to grab my hands and force them onto the dummy. I pull back, but I'm no match for a werewolf. She pushes my hands into the dummy's neck, positioning them so my fingers wrap around the back. Shit. Wait. Is this what I think it is? I glance up at Bennett, my eyes wide. "She was strangled?"

Of course, I get no answer. I'm a suspect. Even my co-worker's cool with treating me like dirt. She packs up and leaves without a second glance at me. I'm about to throw a massive pity party when Bennett reminds me about our prior conversation.

"So, your blood turns vampires human? Does anyone know about this? Outside his parents?"

I nod, wearily. "JR—Juniper Ruth, I mean. Jacob and Saffron Watts. That's it."

"No one else. Not your parents?"

I shake my head.

"So, whoever hit you didn't know that you'd turn Georgina human?"

"Nope."

"Unless Jacob or Saffron came outside after you…"

"Don't. They wouldn't."

His eyes are sad. "I'll look into all this."

And I didn't think I could feel any worse. I sink to a new low. I think I just ruined the lives of my stand-in parents. Shit. I open my mouth to make up some kind of confession. But the door swings open.

CHAPTER 6

Sheila barges into the room carrying more coffee and oh-so-stereotypical-but-delicious donuts. She's an angel of caffeine and mercy.

"Do you accept me as your appointed lawyer?" She gets straight to the point.

"Yeah sure," I respond. That's right. I get an attorney. Idiot. Why have I been sitting here talking to Bennett? Because I'm sleep-deprived. Blood-deprived. Possibly missing some brain matter from that gash in my head.

"Bennett you are no longer allowed to question my client. She and I need the room." Bam.

Bennett tries to give me a reassuring smile but I can't look him in the eyes. He knew I should ask for a lawyer. But he didn't help me. Didn't remind me. He's investigating me. Me!

It makes me feel dirty and angry and offended all over again. I don't care that he is just doing his job. I don't care that I'm being unfair. Right now I just want to kick him. Possibly in the junk. Yeah, I think I'm that mad.

Bennett heads for the door.

"Oh and Bennett?" Sheila adds.

"Yes?" He turns back.

Suddenly one of her snakes pops free of its coil and hisses. Bennett freezes and falls over backward.

"Oh dear," Sheila does not sound at all disturbed. She steps over Bennett and calls into the hall. "Man down. Can we get a little help?" Alfred, a were investigator, pops his head into the room.

"Dang it, Sheila. You know you're supposed to keep those things sedated."

"I know. I know. So sorry. Just got these guys tamed, too." She pats the rogue snake's head as she tucks him back into a braid.

Alfred rolls his eyes and drags Bennett out, bonking the guy's head on the door jamb in the process.

"He shouldn't be out more than five minutes," she calls after

Alfred. "I really did get them done yesterday."

I hold in a laugh, but a snort escapes.

Sheila drags a finger across her throat. She eyes the two-way mirror. "Gonna have to talk to my hairdresser. And by the way guys," she taps on the two-way glass, "my client does not consent to any recording devices or spells of any kind from this point forward."

I imagine I hear a groan from the other side of the glass. Sheila blows the glass a kiss and checks her snakes in the reflection before she closes the door to the room. Then she tosses the bag of donuts to me. "Dig in."

She sits across from me at the table as I down three chocolate donuts and half my coffee in rapid succession.

"So, let's just get started. I've been thinking through arguments for your defense. Technically, we could try to argue double jeopardy. Since she was undead, she was already dead. And the idiot human the Knights hired to kill them so they could transform was caught. He served his time seventy years back. It's risky. Since technically, it wasn't you who killed her the first time."

"I didn't kill her the second time." I'm frickin' indignant. No. Livid. I mean, all I did was pass out. "Apparently it's illegal now to get clubbed and pass out."

"Can you prove that?"

I jut out my lower lip. "What about Bennett's self-defense theory? She attacked me and I fought back."

Sheila stares me straight in the eye. I'm not human, not completely, but her gorgon stare does make my limbs tighten up.

"If you want to argue that, you can. But, then you're a fairy who fights to the death. You know what that means."

The Veil. If I argue that I killed Georgina in self-defense, they won't ever let me cross. Not that seeing my mother is a huge incentive. But, the world beyond the Veil is breathtaking. They don't let darkened souls across. Can I give that up?

"You hesitated," Sheila notices my turmoil. "That's why we don't want to go there unless we absolutely have to. What they have now is circumstantial at best. You were there. She had some of your blood in her system. It's pretty weak evidence. Plus, there are a lotta people out there who have stronger motives than you."

I perk up at that. "Like who?"

Sheila shrugs, her head wrap bobbing as the snakes struggle for balance. "Like her ex."

I use my clueless face to tip her off that more info is necessary.

"Luke Hawkins. That vamp fighting Bennett at the time of the murder."

Hot Vamp?! Hot Vamp was dating that vicious vein-eating bitch? I shake my head as my opinion of him drops a notch or two.

"Bennett's thinking about Jacob or Saffron too." I pitch in. "We have to protect them too."

Sheila sighs. "A seat on the City Council is pretty good motive. A lotta power in this town."

"They wouldn't do it."

"Kid, I know. But their heads aren't on the chopping block right now. Let's worry about you."

There's a knock at the door. Jerry sticks his head in. He's the bailiff, a troll with a lot of muscle to keep order in the courtroom. He gives an apologetic half-smile.

"Gotta take you up for arraignment, Miss Fox."

I sigh and stand brushing donut crumbs off of my rumpled clothes. "Don't I get a shower?"

He shakes his head.

"Apparently murder suspects don't get the same right to cleanliness other prisoners do."

Sheila pats my hand. "Don't worry. They can't hold you."

I pad to the door and give Sheila a sad little wave. I'm going to the courtroom for the second time in twenty-four hours. Only this time, I'm gonna be sitting in the pen.

Jerry takes my arm gently and leads me to the elevator, which we ride to the very top floor. To the felony courtroom.

I've been to probably a hundred arraignments. But never my own. My heart pounds in my chest even though I know that this is a nothing court hearing.

The felony courtroom is Saffron's courtroom. And she's going to have to announce to the world that I've been charged with murder. My stomach churns. It feels like someone turned the AC too high because suddenly my arms are covered in goosebumps.

Jerry pulls open the door.

I almost pee myself in relief. Saffron is not on the bench. She must've recused herself since I was on the docket. Instead little red Ruddy is wearing the black robes today.

Jerry has me shuffle over to the defendants' box. I notice I'm the only defendant, and I wonder for a second if Ruddy's giving me the same kind of treatment he gave the peeping grandma. If so, I'm grateful to be spared the humiliation.

Bella represents the prosecution. Great.

Sheila scrambles through the door at the last second and

stands at my defense. But Sheila brings with her two people I really don't want to see right now. Bennett and Hot Vamp. Luke Hawkins.

Is it totally pathetic that for a second I forget about the life-altering importance of court and just curse the fact that I'm a smelly unwashed, unholy mess in front of two of the hottest guys I've ever seen in my life?

Why are they here? Why isn't JR here? Where's Jacob?

Judge Ruddy bangs his gavel. He gestures to Hot Vamp and Bennett. "This be a closed courtroom this mornin' gents. I'll need to be asking you to leave, lessin' you be here on official business that this."

Luke Hawkins grins. "Your Honor, I'm here to post the bond for Ms. Lyon Fox." My eyes grow wide. Who the heck is this guy? The murder vic's ex wants to post my bond? We just met yesterday! Does he know how guilty that makes me look right now?

I turn to Sheila to share a look of disbelief, but she has a smug little grin on her face.

Why would she be happy? Oh, right. She said something about motive. Why is this guy so dang happy Georgina's gone? Unless he did it.

BELLA SPEAKS. "YOUR HONOR, THE DA'S OFFICE WOULD LIKE to approach the bench."

Wait, what? My suspicious eval of Hot Vamp halts. This is an arraignment. A quick calendar court hearing. Why could she possibly want to approach?

Bella smiles at me and continues. "Exculpatory evidence has come to light. Our chief investigator, Bennett French, is available to speak to you about this evidence in chambers."

Sheila insists. "Your Honor, I would like to be a part of this conversation, particularly as my client was held without being read her rights or formally charged." She's total sweetness and composure. But she had been on a tear when I ate her donuts. Something about habeas corpus and rights. Junk that I don't even know about as a paralegal. By the time it gets to me, a case is already filed and moving. I hope she goes up there and gives them an earful. But I watch her approach, meek as a mouse.

Ruddy eyes her and Bennett. Then he jerks his head to a black door on the back wall. He exits the bench, and he, Sheila, and Bennett disappear behind the door for a few minutes.

My eyes stay glued to that door. I don't know if my heart even beats. The rest of me is frozen in anticipation. I feel like my heart is too.

Ruddy comes back. He takes the bench. I'm so nervous I could wet myself.

"In light of new evidence this mornin', I'm releasin' Ms. Fox on her own recognizance. Ms. Fox, your arraignment is delayed two weeks. You must appear in court for your new arraignment. In the meantime, you canna' leave town, lass."

I exhale and have to grab the little wooden wall of the pen as my knees give out.

Jerry smiles and opens the gate to the main courtroom. I rush out of the pen.

I hug Sheila. She lets me, despite the smell, which just makes me like her a little more. I run to hug Bennett but Bella steps into my path and glances meaningfully at Ruddy and Hot Vamp. I mean Luke. Luke Hawkins. Now my prime suspect. The man who wanted to pay for a supposed killer to walk free.

Bella's meaning is clear. (Which is crazy because I don't have that pack-mind talky thing.) Her eyes say, 'Talk to Luke.' She just delayed the case against me. I guess I owe her. A little. I turn and saunter over to Luke.

"Thanks for having my back."

"Not a problem. I was kind of looking forward to seeing you in a jumpsuit."

I look down, remembering I haven't showered. Gross. Ew.

Dammit. In my elation, I forgot how disgusting I am. I mean, he can probably smell my breath! I quickly back up a few steps. "Sorry. Guess us big-time criminals don't get the same posh treatment as you little guys."

He laughs. Damn. That's a nice sound. Especially to my newly free ears.

"Why don't you shower at home, and then I'll pick you up and take you to breakfast somewhere. Since, you know, I couldn't bond you out."

I smile and bite my lip, glancing surreptitiously at Bennett. He gives a tiny nod. He wants me to go on a date with a hot suspect? A hot *murder* suspect. Isn't he afraid for me? Gah! Jerk.

CHAPTER 7

I give Luke my address and tell him to meet me there in an hour. Because I don't want to subject some poor witch to smelling me, I walk home. It takes about ten minutes to get to my front door. I'm slipping the key into the lock when the knob turns and the door is jerked open from the inside.

JR pulls me in to a monster hug. Then she pushes me inside where Jacob and Saffron are waiting.

"Oh my stars. You smell worse than that burnt meatloaf Arnold brought to work last week!" JR exclaims.

"Thanks."

Saffron wrinkles her nose. "Yeah, go hop in the shower."

"Wait a second, Ms. Bossy. How come none of you were at

the courthouse crying and wringing your hands over me? I'm very offended. This wasn't like some were-barking violation or something. They accused me of murder!"

Jacob steps in to take the brunt of my ire. Which is brave. Because there's a lot. These are supposed to be my peeps. "Look. Bennett told us it would be best if we all came here—"

"Why is everyone in the world listening to Bennett? Like he's some master of the universe? I was knocked out and I was his best suspect for murder."

"Not my best," a gravelly voice said from behind.

I whirled around to see my ex in my doorway. "What are you doing here? Stalker. Ruddy let me out on OR. And Sheila's gonna eat Bella's booty for unlawful holding. Maybe yours too. It's over."

"Unfortunately, it's not. There's still a murder investigation open."

"Okay." I tilt my head and raise my eyebrows, wondering why the heck he's still here.

"I'd also like to clarify, for everyone else's benefit, I'm not a stalker."

I roll my eyes. JR giggles until I death-glare her into silence. Best friends are supposed to back a girl up. "Your friend card is in serious jeopardy right now," I tell her.

"So's yours." She jerks her head at the myriad of dead plants around my living room.

"Fine. We're even. But only if you kick the stalker out while I shower."

I stomp to my bedroom like a five-year-old.

"Did you mean kick him out of the living room into your bedroom?" JR crows after me. "Cause I can do that."

Everyone dissolves into laughter behind me. I flip them all off.

AFTER A SHOWER, THREE ROUNDS OF BRUSHING MY TEETH, AND life-reaffirming hot cocoa from Jacob, I feel alive again. I'm sitting on my couch, dressed for my date with Luke in a cute little black tank and skirt, and listening to—of all people— Bennett. Because JR did not kick him out.

"Just listen, he's got a plan," she says.

Saffron and Jacob back her up. So basically, I'm peer-pressured into listening to the plan of the man who arrested me.

Bennett's brilliant plan is for me to wear the spelled version of a wire while I talk to Hot Vamp.

"Because a guy I just met yesterday is gonna trip all over himself to confess murder to me."

Bennett frowns. "He was tripping all over himself to bond you out. You should have seen him running around the courthouse."

That makes me pause. I picture the image. Hot muscled vamp running from courtroom to courtroom, desperate to save his beloved. Sweat dripping down his brow, fear etched on his face. He gasps out in a southern accent, 'Is she here? The beautiful girl they want for murder?' Because somehow my melodramatic fantasies always make people have southern accents.

Bennett is snapping his fingers in front of my face to bring me back to reality.

"Maybe you shouldn't go to breakfast."

I wave his hand away like a pesky fly. "Maybe you should give me a break. I got hit on the head, drank, and accused of murder."

JR rolls her eyes. "How long are you gonna use that one as an excuse?"

"Forever."

"You get two weeks. Tops. Then I'm gonna sing the not-listening song whenever you pull that."

"Noted."

"Ladies, can we focus?"

Bennett looks like he wants to pull his hair out. That makes me happy. I want to pull his hair out. But then that thought makes me think about pulling his hair. Which makes me horny. Oh no. "I am having problems thinking straight right now." I'm a little giddy. Can that be an after-effect of shock? Or is it an after-effect of three donuts, two coffees, and a hot cocoa? Or an after-effect of being charged with murder and then getting out of jail? Or a fore-effect of having a spy-date with a possible murderer? See … my brain cells are really fried.

Bennett's in my face, pleading baby boy look in full force. "He'll be here in five minutes, okay? Five minutes. I just need you to last an hour after that. I've got this spelled necklace for you to wear. It'll record everything you say, play it for me back at the office. Okay?"

I take the necklace from him. It's a dingy-looking old penny with a hole drilled into it and a crap chain that will probably leave a green trail on my skin. I look at JR. "I told you this guy's a stalker."

"I'm not—"

JR nods, playing along. It's why we're besties. "Totally a stalker."

"He wants to hear me make out with a vamp."

"You said you'd never touch—" Bennett's tone gets terse. His mouth crinkles to one side. He's totally got a pout face.

I laugh. "OMG. I won't. But you got all riled up."

"I'm not riled up."

"You seem a little upset." JR chimes in. Jacob and Saffron work to control their smiles.

I turn to JR. "But not like murderous stalker upset, right?"

She pretends to evaluate him. "I dunno."

"Are you gonna wear the damn necklace or not?"

I roll my eyes and slip it over my head. Spoilsport. Bennett always has to take things so seriously. "He's gonna notice. Or suspect. If he's such a bad guy that you're supposedly stalking him, not me, then he probably has a dozen runes in those tattoos that will render this worthless."

But, that gives me an idea. "One sec." I scurry to my bedroom and pull out a tiny hairclip spy-cam I got a few years back from Jacob. Picture quality sucks, so I've never used it. But it'll grab audio and some kind of video. I put the clip in my hair. Kinda cheesy. But not spelled. A lot of people in the magic world don't think about human gadgets. So maybe this backup will work.

There's a knock at my door. Shit. He's here.

"Everyone into my bedroom. Now!" I stage-whisper, tripping over my own feet as I go to the door.

I wait until they're hidden. Then I pull open the door with a staged grin. Luke Hawkins, hot vamp extraordinaire, is wearing a yummy leather jacket and tight black jeans and standing on my stoop. I mentally curse the number of people huddled in my bedroom. Not that I could drag him in there. But if I could … okay brain. Cooperate. Words. Job. Evidence. Go.

I hold the door open for Luke to enter. "Hey! Come in—one-time invitation only."

He grins. "Someone's read the vamp manual."

"Yeah well, I have a problem with ex-boyfriends turning into stalkers," I say loudly. There Bennett. Take that. In fact, that gives me an idea. I think I know how to get Luke to open up and bug Bennett at the same time. Ha ha. My brain might not be so far gone after all.

"Let me grab a jacket and purse and we can get outta here." I get a grey cropped jacket from the hall closet but forget the contents of my purse were dumped into an evidence envelope. "Sorry. One sec." I dump the envelope onto my counter. I pick out the essentials and toss them into a clutch.

I turn to see Luke staring at the dead plants. "What—" he gestures.

"I like dead things." I wink and twirl, letting my skirt ride up a little. I mean, can't hurt to loosen his tongue with a little flirting right?

He trails behind me like a puppy. I smile and lock my door.

"What about your rule about touching?"

I bite my lip and give him a naughty grin. "There's an exception to every rule, you know. You wanna be my exception?" I start down the stairs. I glance up. He's practically salivating. Good. Yay. Oh my. His face. Those burning blue eyes. I better be careful, or I'll be salivating too and this fake date will turn into a very real date. A very dangerous date. For both of us.

I turn away to catch my breath. Damn. It's been way too long since I played the field if I can't control myself around murder suspects. "Where are we headed?" I gesture down the street, where streetlights outshine the stars. A couple of neighbors, gremlins with a crying kid, wave as they walk by.

"You're fae, yeah?" Luke gestures to the blue jewel on my chin.

I nod.

"I thought we'd do something for that sweet tooth, then. Wendel's is supposed to have—"

"Cinnamon rolls!" Mmm. I could kiss him. That sounds perfect. Bennett used to take me to Wendels whenever I was having a bad day. It's the world's cutest fifties diner.

"You know them?"

"They are the epitome of drenched-in-butter happiness! I think you chose well, fang boy."

He smiles.

I smile. Shit. Focus. You're a spy. A spy. I take a deep breath, then take his arm as we start to walk to our destination. I have to tell my vamp panic-meter to calm down. It's not really touching. It's through leather. It's fine. We're on a busy street. I need him comfortable. I'm pretending to be normal. Deep breath. Deep deep breath.

"Rule one. I touch you only."

He nods. "Whatever you want." He opens his mouth to ask, but I cut him off.

"Not ready to talk about it yet." Not eager to share that my blood could humanize him in case he happens to be a crazy killer who has a wish list of victims in his sock drawer. Don't want him draining me in order to make that job easier. I want him to think whatever happened to Georgina was a pure freak-of-nature accident.

"Okay, need a fun fact about you." It's my fave first date game.

"What's a fun fact?"

"Okay I'll start. Fun fact: when I was fifteen my mom hired a witch to curse me so that I cannot actually ever curse out loud. She thought it wasn't ladylike."

"Seriously? That sounds pretty awful."

"Oh it was. Imagine being a teenager with all that pent-up rage and all I could call my mother was son of a beached whale. So not cool when everybody's laughing at you and you're really ticked and then it just makes you wanna laugh. Which makes you even more mad."

"Did you ever get the curse lifted?"

I shake my head. "Tried. Can't. I have a little arsenal of newbie curses. I can say things like mofo. Eff. All the texty acronyms. But the closest I can get to some are shizzle."

"I don't know how I can top that. Okay… Fun fact about me. I've been a vamp for eighty years, I've lived in Tres Lunas for sixty-five of those years, I worked down at the shipyard—"

I interrupt. "No no no. Those are not fun facts. Those are the opposite of fun facts. Those are boring facts. Try again."

"You want something embarrassing, don't you?"

I stop walking and wait until he reluctantly stops and turns to face me. My grin is the size of Montana. "Oh, yes I do. And by the look on your face, it's going to be a good one."

Luke bites his lip and looks totally delicious. He sighs. "Alright. I like … smelling food."

I shrug. "Who doesn't?"

He turns so we start walking again. "Most vamps try to shed

as much of their humanity as possible. You know, embrace the power, get rid of human weakness."

"Wow. Wait. So, like guilty pleasure scale, how bad are you?" I glance over. If a vamp could blush, I think Luke would be blushing. "OMG." I lean in. "Is it like a fetish?"

"No. Not. Not quite."

I raise an eyebrow.

"I said no."

"You're lying!"

"Your turn," he's gruff.

"Specific foods or any food? Like standard drizzled chocolate or more crazy? Like if I covered myself in cookie dough?"

His shakes his head and won't maintain eye contact. "Your turn," I said.

I giggle. "This is by far the best game of fun facts I've ever played. And I had someone confess to me once that he went through a streaking phase. Like he loved half-shifting and flying naked past the neighbors."

"Frat bat-shifter?"

I laugh. "Something like that." I hope Bennett's listening in with his co-workers right now. And I hope that made him really uncomfortable. It still doesn't make up for what he did to me. Not by a long shot. I decide he needs to be a little more uncomfortable, since Luke and I are still a block away from the restaurant.

"So, I have a problem and I need some male advice."

"The problem you had earlier this evening?"

"Georgina Knight's murder?" I gauge his face carefully as I say this. I'm not an expert, but I think he looks sad. "No. Not that. I don't even know where to start with that."

He sighs. "Me either."

I raise an eyebrow. "Did you know her?"

He nods. "We dated a while ago."

"Oh." Well, that's a way more honest answer than I expected. But then, you can't exactly hide dating someone can you? "I'm sorry."

He shrugs. "We weren't a match."

I lean in and whisper, "She wasn't a foodie?"

He gives a half-laugh. "Definitely not."

I wink. "Lucky thing I am."

His eyes glint in the moonlight. "I hope so. So, what's your problem?"

"An ex problem."

Luke's eyebrows shoot up.

"This guy is stalking me."

"Have you called the police?"

I sigh. "Not like provable stalking."

We turn a corner and Wendel's is there. You can smell the deliciousness from outside. It doesn't even need a sign. In a town full of were animals with keen noses, the smells coming from this place are better than flashing neon. Cinnamon rolls early. Barbeque later. And strawberries if you get there just before dawn and they're making homemade jam. Sometimes I sit out on the curb and just inhale. (For a minute. Before I go in to stuff my face.)

We walk in. It's not midnight yet so there's no lunch crowd. The typical fifties black and white tiles decorate the floor. Red booths line the room. A giant glass-faced bakery display tempts everyone in line to add four hundred calories to their order.

But my favorite are the posters. Wendels has posters of all the monster movies that came out in the fifties. *Dracula. Creature from the Black Lagoon. The Mole People.* There's nothing funnier than seeing what humans think we look like. Edging the posters are polaroids of customers mocking the poses. Vamps pretending to be Dracula ... you get the idea.

Luke and I are silent while we're in line. But it's not awkward. Which in itself is weird. Shouldn't I feel more uncomfortable? I just met this guy. Bennett thinks he might be a murderer. I should be on edge, right? But it feels like we're old friends. Do I have broken bad-guy radar? Or is he so hot that the wires in my brain have literally short circuited? I have no idea but staring at him out of the corner of my eye is so frickin' enjoyable.

I'm tempted to see if he wants to take a polaroid just so I can sneak back later and steal it. Hide it under my pillow. (Because vamps totally show up in pics now. At least the ones with enough coin to purchase a spell or two from Wishmart.)

Before I can fully form a reasonable way to ask for photos, we reach the front of the line.

I order. They do have a waitress claiming she's AB negative on the menu but Luke waves her off.

"Are you sure?" I look at the massive, head-sized cinnamon roll and giant cup of milk I'm about to consume. "I might feel more comfortable if you ate something too. Instead of just staring at me."

He laughs. "First, your cinnamon roll smells delicious." He winks. "Second, I think staring at you is my new favorite thing."

I roll my eyes. "Yeah, because before now, I have looked so amazing."

"I liked your skirt in court," he responds as we sit at a corner booth. He scoots over until we're as close as possible without actual touching. My body hums in fear but also in awareness.

His comment prompts an entire diatribe against Arnold and Bennett, and an explanation of my under-the-desk filing antics that has Hot Vamp's shoulders shaking in laughter. He's not a murderer. No one who gets my jokes could possibly be a bad person.

"Would you, as a guy, ever try to get a job at your ex's office?"

His eyes widen. "Stalker didn't just show up. He's working at your office?"

I nod.

He's quiet for a minute. "You're over this guy, right?"

"We broke up over two years ago." I roll my eyes and try and sound nonchalant. I do not want to mention how many recent months I've spent crying over that relationship, or how every date until today's spy date with a laughing, hot-as-hell potential murderer fizzled in comparison to Bennett.

Luke's hand reaches for mine, but he stops himself. His fingers hover centimeters away. His stare is intense. "I'm glad you're over him. If he's following you, I don't think he's over you. Because I have to tell you, the only way in hell I'd subject myself to working with an ex is if I wanted her back."

I drop my fork.

CHAPTER 8

I excuse myself to go to the ladies' room, but really, I just
need a breather after that bombshell.

He's wrong. Luke's wrong. I only brought this topic up to
piss Bennett off if he was listening. And now, here I am
having a hard time breathing.

It's not true—

My cell rings.

"Hello."

"Where are you? What's happening?" Bennett's voice is tense
on the line.

"I'm in the flipping ladies room. What's your problem?"

"My problem is you're messing around. Flirting. Talking

about me. Don't think I don't know what you're doing. You're not getting information."

"Well, my problem is you shouldn't even be working at my office. I shouldn't even be accused of murder."

"Damn it, Ly, I'm trying to help you. I got enough evidence to let them bond you out on OR. Do you even know what bond normally is on a murder case? Now, I'm trying to keep you safe from—"

"From a guy who seems nice and normal and not a stalker?"

"From a guy who was following Georgina the night she was murdered who has known associations with the Crypts."

I still. The Crypts are bad news. A local mostly-vamp gang who like to bury their victims alive.

Wait. "He was following Georgina?" He said he was over her …

Bennett notes my silence. "Finally, you're taking this seriously."

I snap. "Finally, you're giving me some mother-lovin' info and not treating me like I'm four."

"I wouldn't treat you like you're four if you didn't act like you were four."

I want to throw my phone at the wall. I resist, reminding myself I'm still on leave until this entire investigation closes.

I can't afford a new phone. Instead of destroying my cell, I end the call and do the next best thing. I pull off Bennett's necklace and drop it in the toilet. I flush. I hope he can hear that sound back at the office and I hope it sounds like an effin' tidal wave.

I touch up my lipstick and go back to my date.

I slide into our booth and say, "Sorry. You kinda freaked me out I guess."

Luke smiles softly. "I noticed. Sorry."

I push back my half-eaten cinnamon roll and stare at a three-year-old centaur with palamino coloring whose parents seem to have given her the run of the place. They're nowhere in sight. She smacks another patron with a spoon. A little whirlwind of chaos. A mini-me.

I let the silence linger for a second, deciding to try to pull some more of the innocent girl-needs-help thing. It seems better than the alternative, which is hitting him for lying and saying he's over his ex when he isn't and then giving me the best date I've had in years. Oh. Shit. Calm down. Game face. Go.

"What do I do about this guy? How do I let him know I'm not interested? What would work if it was you?"

He laughs. "This is the craziest first date conversation I've ever had."

"Me too. But I need help. I'll let you sniff my cinnamon roll." I push the plate toward him and bat my eyes.

"I wish you didn't mean that literally."

"Dirty mind! I thought you liked it literally."

"Not nearly as much as the alternative."

"But seriously. I don't want him to keep following me. But I don't want to be mean. Too mean. I have to work with him now."

"Well, that's where you and my ex differ."

"What?"

Luke runs his free hand through his hair. "She had no problems being mean."

I gasp, as if I didn't know Georgina was an ice queen. "Who would ever want to get rid of you? She's crazy. I mean look at those tattoos." Licking my lips is totally a seductive ploy. It has nothing to do with the way his biceps bulge as he puts his elbows on the table. Nothing.

He laughs. "They're great right? Okay, okay. Stop. Or I'll have to wipe drool off your face, and no touching, right?"

He's serious. I am about to drool. It's bad.

"Georgina is—was crazy. I still can't believe it." He sighs. "She had a plan for her life. Most vamps live so long and they embrace a purpose. Usually become a little fanatical about it.

I didn't fit her image for City Council boy-toy so she didn't want me anymore."

"That's a stupendous reason to dump someone. Cursing curse. You know what I mean." I wave a hand.

"That's what I thought."

"You should have argued with her over it. I would have."

"I was going to argue with her. That's why I was there last night."

Luke was following her. He admitted it. Bennett was telling the truth. He was probably telling the truth about the Crypts too. Shit. I try not to tense.

The centaur toddler runs over to me, holding her spoon up like a sword. Here's a quick out. Distraction strike.

"One sec. I can't resist." I unroll Luke's unused napkin and grab the spoon. "On guard." She squeals and smacks my wrist with her spoon. Clearly, she has not yet perfected her silverware battle technique. I give her a pass. Until she opens her mouth. Puke spews directly at me. I jump sideways, right into Luke's lap. I escape the stream, but now I'm caught in his brawny arms.

"I—I—" I try not to panic.

"Well. This is a memorable first date. Think that's the first time a girl's ever literally jumped me."

I can't help it. I laugh. Loud. Hard. Here I am in the arms of a real-life scary vamp probable-criminal and I just escaped a puke attack. Tears stream down my face. "I think I just ruined my makeup."

"I'd offer to help but I think—"

His comment reminds me that I'm touching him. That I'm still on his lap. I scramble over him to the non-puke side of the booth. "Sorry."

I eye the damage. Only thing is, it doesn't look like damage at all. Where the little girl spewed, there's raspberry-colored whipped cream. And it smells like...

"Is that ... chocolate chip cookies?" Luke's longing is evident in his voice. His eyes are closed. Rapture is the only word to describe his expression.

"Freshly puked." I counter.

His eyes pop open. He eyes the mess. "That's just wrong."

"I know."

There are a couple shifters in dog form across the room, lapping up some spilled ice cream. I'd prefer not to be here when they see the mess that the wild child left behind. Luke and I stand.

"Sorry about all that weirdness."

"I'm not." He waggles his eyebrows suggestively.

I shake my head at him. "Don't. You just told me you were following your ex last night." Despite being scared of vamps, part of me is a little sad. "You aren't over her. You aren't ready for dating. Which means now I have to go home and pout and have dreams about those biceps."

He stares at me hard. "No. I'm very over her. She dumped me two months ago. When she decided to start this stupid campaign. I was going to argue with her last night because she dumped me so she could steal her best friend's boyfriend like the lying, back-stabbing bitch she was. Cherry just told me last night. And she was devastated."

Wait, Georgina stole her best friend's boyfriend? That's an epic low. And that puts someone new in the hot seat. Someone who might have a more urgent motive to kill her.

"Who's her best friend?"

"Cherry Jones, the baker who just made that cinnamon roll you ate. She owns this place."

I groan. Wendel's is one of my top three favorite places in the city. "If she did it and has to close up shop, I'm gonna kill her."

But first, I better find out if she did.

CHAPTER 9

I turn to Luke. "Introduce me, please."

"What—now?" he asks.

I shove away my anxiety about touching vamps to push on his back. I take zero notice of his ripped trapezius muscles. The shiver down my spine is completely out of fear as I steer him toward the kitchen door. "Yes, now. I've been accused of murder and her best friend probably knows every single person who hates her. She probably knows exactly who did it."

If someone ever decided to do me in, you bet JR would have a list of suspects. And in this case, Georgina's best friend is now one of *my* top suspects.

Luke ducks to the side and stops before we enter the kitchen.

"Maybe we shouldn't talk to her if the police haven't talked to her first."

He's got a point. Dammit. "What if we just ask her about people Georgina ticked off lately? We won't mention exactly what happened last night."

No way in the underworld am I walking out those doors without finding out what she knows. Best friends always have dirt. And this one has even more than most. She has hate too. I push Luke through the kitchen doors, ignoring a waitress who tries to stop us.

"Cherry?" I call out at the top of my voice. It's not loud enough. A working kitchen is loud: knives, and hissing pots, and yelling orders. I ninja around a couple of sous chefs to get to what looks like the bakery section.

I bump into a woman with the rainbow-colored hair typical of a unicorn shifter. She turns around and bats the biggest violet eyes I've ever seen.

"Can I help you?"

Luke catches up in time to make the introduction. "Cherry, this is Ly-Ly. I met her last night."

I have trouble believing this sweet, innocent looking chef was BFF with Georgina.

I grab her flour-covered hand. "I'm in love with your cream puffs, your cinnamon rolls, and pretty much every fruit tart you make. Except kiwi. Not my thing. I just had to meet you when he said he knew you." I pour on the flattery, which isn't hard, because it's all one hundred percent true. She's a kitchen goddess.

She blushes. "Thanks. Have you tried the new pixie-berry scones?"

"No! They didn't even tell me about it out front!"

"They smell like heaven," Luke pitches in.

Cherry smiles at Luke. "I tolerate him because he's at least half-appreciative of my work." She waves an arm and I notice scars down her forearm, in a crisscross pattern.

"Ouch!" I touch her arm again. "I have a couple scars like that." I try not to be obvious about studying her scratch marks. A couple are fresh. I'll have to tell Bennett. If there was a struggle between Georgina and her killer, the killer could have as many scars as I do. Is Cherry mad enough for murder?

"Yes, well, the price of working in the kitchen." She pats her arm. "I like to think of them as battle wounds."

"Well, it's definitely worth the sacrifice. If food could be in a museum, yours would have one," I assure her. "I'll get the scones next time I come in."

"Great!" She blinks, not quite sure what to do with us. I'm trying to find some smooth segue when Luke jumps in.

"I saw Georgina last night."

Immediately, Cherry's temper flares. "What'd that bitch have to say for herself?"

"I couldn't really talk to her. I got jumped."

"Oh my gosh. Are you okay? Was Timmy there? Is he okay? Did you talk to him?" I didn't think it was possible for a human shifter's eyes to get so wide. But it's almost like she's a cartoon. Her eyes keep growing and growing, until they overpower her face. She blinks back tears. It's a sucker punch to the gut. Irresistible cuteness and worry rolled up into one. Damn. I've heard about unicorn powers before. But Cherry is beyond. I want to do anything to help her. Anything to stop her lip from quivering.

"Timmy wasn't there last night. I didn't see him." I pat her arm, trying to see the scars again. No luck.

My reassurance helps slightly. Luke's nod helps more. Her eyes grow more normal-sized. "He really wasn't there?" She tilts her head. "But he wasn't at home."

Luke shrugs. "Georgina kinda went on a rampage last night."

Cherry rolls her eyes. "What else is new?"

"Well, kind of a public rampage," I add. "She accused Saffron Watts of leaking stuff to the press about her."

Cherry sighed. "Like what?"

"Draining a human."

She runs a hand through her hair, dulling the rainbow with flour. "Of course. You know, she brings all this stuff on herself. She's been acting weird since this campaign started."

"What you mean?" I ask, leaning casually against her worktable, ignoring an assistant baker who glares at me.

"Well, for starters, she stopped letting anybody go over to her apartment about two months ago. I mean, Georgina used to host the most awesome dinner parties in town. Half because I made the food, of course. Does it make sense that she stopped right before she wanted to campaign for City Council? It's weird."

If I've learned anything from watching the investigators at our office, it's agree with people to keep them talking. "That is *really* weird. They would make such easy campaign fundraisers."

"That's what I told her!" Cherry says. She sighs. "But what do I know? Except how to pick a boyfriend that trots off the second Georgina snaps her fingers."

Luke pulls her into a hug.

I try to add to the sense of solidarity by saying, "Well Timmy must be blind because you're way better-looking than Georgina."

Cherry looks up at me and sniffs. "Thanks. I told him, she's ruthless. She only wants him for his horn."

I'm shocked. I'm embarrassed that she mentioned *it* at work. In front of one of her assistants.

Luke whispers in Cherry's ear. Then they both are laughing. Like deep belly-laughing, staring right at me. Which of course, does not make me a happy camper.

"What in the hizzle are you guys laughing at?"

My pseudo-curse just makes Luke wheeze until he's clutching his knees. Even Cherry stops to watch him lose it.

"Okay, now I'm lost," she says. She turns to me, because Luke is still bent over, gasping. "Your face on the horn thing. You know what our horns are good for, right?"

"Don't," Luke begs, hand swinging out to grab hers. "Don't ruin her innocence."

"Innocence my ass. She was thinking dirty things."

That's it. My face is officially magma red. I think it's on fire.

"If you shave a bit off our horn, and mix it into food, you can make people forget."

"Forget what?"

"Whatever you want. There's a spell or something that goes with it."

"Okay. So, she wanted Timmy's horn?"

Cherry nods. "She asked me first. But I turned her down. No freaking way I'm losing my job over something shady."

I nod. Memory-loss curses carry a hefty fine and minimum of three months in the dungeon. "I don't blame you. But why would she want to make someone forget? Who's that mad at her?"

Luke finally rejoins the conversation. "Well, if she got accused of draining, that would be something she'd want people to forget pretty quick."

Cherry nods. "Could be that. Could be whatever's been going down at her apartment. She could have wanted to spell her opponent into forgetting about the race."

I pale.

The Saffron I know has always been strict. Self-denial, hard work, honesty, integrity. Those are her mantras.

Georgina's attack the other night was random. I replay it in my head. I remember thinking Georgina might've wanted to cast a spell. Did she have some shaved horn? Did she try? Did Saffron find out? My stomach drops.

No. I don't really believe Saffron could be capable of something like this. Even if Georgina did find a spell and Saffron found out, Saffron was still inside. There are witnesses. Bennett interviewed everyone, right?

Luke pulls out his cell. "Both of you look really upset about this whole prospect. Look let's call Timmy to see what's going on. Cherry, you can talk to him. Clear this all up. You'll hear there was no horn shaving. And this paranoid theory you two have going will be over."

Cherry nods and wipes her fingers on her apron. "I should check on him anyway. He didn't call me back last night." She dials.

I hold my breath. And keep holding. Holding. I hear a beep.

"Timmy, it's Cherry. Call me when you get this. I just want to know you're okay." She hangs up, eyes wide as a doll's again. "He's not answering. He wasn't at his place last night. He's missing."

I turn to stare at Luke.

Either Timmy the unicorn is missing, or he found out about Georgina's plan for his horn. What if he didn't agree? What if he didn't just say no like Cherry? What if he got mad, killed Georgina, and is now on the run?

My list of suspects just keeps growing.

CHAPTER 10

L uke wants to walk me back to my apartment, but I won't let him. I stop in front of Wendel's and turn to him.

"Things are just really messed up right now. I'm accused of murder. You have an open case. You have an ex you're not over."

Luke opens his mouth to protest but I hold up a hand.

"Let me finish. I really like you. And your biceps. More than I've liked anyone in years. And that is really hard for me to say. Because I have avoided vampires for almost a decade."

"Why?" Luke asks.

"Because I'm bad for you."

"Maybe I like bad girls."

I give a weak smile. "Look. I'm not saying never. I'm just saying not yet. I think we both have a couple things that we need to work through first."

"But—"

"Don't. Believe me it is taking all the self-control I have to walk away right now. I mean who goes through a first date involving puke and still thinks it's awesome? And it was awesome."

Luke tentatively reaches out his hand. Trembling I reach mine out until our fingers just brush. It's scary and electric all at once.

"You need to know something about me," Luke steps closer. "Earlier I mentioned vampire obsessions." His eyes flicker back and forth between mine and he leans forward slowly. He whispers, "I think I just found a new one."

SHIVERS OF GLEE FOLLOW ME ON MY WALK HOME. I LOOK BACK once before I turn the corner, and Luke's still standing there in the moonlight, staring at me. OMG. I may not have actual wings, but I totally feel like I'm flying. Which is insane, considering the last twenty-four hours. My little bubble of glee pops the second I reach my doorstep and reach into my clutch for my keys.

"Mother Eff! Where the duck are they? Did I seriously leave my keys inside my apartment?" Grunting and groaning I walk downstairs to Mrs. Snow's apartment. I inhale a big whiff of something curry-like as I knock on her door. It's a better smell than most nights she tries to play witch-doctor, so I guess at least there's that.

Mrs. Snow's door swings open. But instead of Mrs. Snow, a familiar little old lady glares up at me. It's Tabitha Blue, the sneaky little peeper from Ruddy's courtroom. She looks as shocked to see me as I am to see her.

Luckily, Mrs. Snow barges up to the door and shoulders her out of the way, ending the awkward staring. Sarah Snow's a true-blue southern belle who's never met someone she doesn't consider a friend. It's unfortunate her potion-making skills are so atrocious. Otherwise, I wouldn't mind visiting her. As it is though, I try not to look concerned as blue smoke curls around the two women.

Mrs. Snow waves away the smoke with a grin. "Lyon. Lost your keys again, huh? Girl, you really oughtta let me spell those things so they're glued to your hand."

"Told you I had a bad experience with that."

"Well come on in, sugar! We're just settin' down fer tea."

My stomach is so full of cinnamon roll that I almost groan but it is not a good idea to turn down a southern Nisse's hospitality. Especially one who's holding your keys. Nisse are related to brownies, helpful and sweet creatures, until you cross them. I make it a point never to cross Mrs. Snow. So I enter the widow's apartment, sliding past Tabitha Blue with a polite nod.

"Saw you leave with that handsome fella'. You have a date, sugar-pie?" Snow asks as she putters around her duck-themed kitchen.

"Yup." I slide into a barstool.

"Well now, isn't that nice?" She winks and slides me a tea-cup with a goose's neck for a handle. "Tabby, bring your tea on in here!"

Tabby comes into the room reluctantly, clearly suspicious of me.

"I'm Lyon. Nice to meet you." I hold out my hand and Tabby shakes, but the look behind her thick glasses is threatening. She must not want her crystal ball habits known in her social circles. Fine by me. I don't really want Mrs. Snow knowing I've been accused of murder. (Falsely, but still.)

When Mrs. Snow's back is turned I mime zipping my lips and Tabby relaxes.

"You said you had a bad experience with a sticking spell once?" She seizes on the only thing she knows about me to start a conversation.

"My mom. She was a little bit of a control freak. She was

worried about me getting lost so she had a spell done to make me stick with my cousin. Boy cousin. She did not specify anything about releases. Or exceptions. So you can imagine what happened when I had to go to the bathroom."

Mrs. Snow returns with her own cup of tea so full of sugar it's practically sludge. In true southern fashion, she has an appropriately dramatic response for my story. "No. She didn't. You poor thing!"

Tabby yowls in laughter. "Mightta' even been more traumatic for your cousin, poor guy."

"My mom had to stand between us with a sheet every time … for two days. That's how long it took this shoddy spell caster to come up with an antidote. I mean. Who does that? Sell something and not know the antidote? Never again."

Mrs. Snow pats my hand. "Can't say I blame you, dear."

Tabby interjects, "So now you just what? Lose your keys. You should get a crystal ball you know. Easiest way to look for lost things."

"That's a good idea."

"I brought mine if you want to have a quick look-see. Sarah and I were just gonna—"

"Gonna look for a potion ingredient I lost dear," Mrs. Snow's interjection seems suspicious. Almost too quick.

I raise my eyebrows at Tabby. She gives me the same

innocent old-grandma look she gave Ruddy. And I know. She and Mrs. Snow were gonna spy on male shifters! My disgust and admiration at this revelation is suddenly overshadowed. I put two and two together. I turn to Tabby.

"I'd love to have your help with the crystal ball. But not looking for keys. I'm looking for a friend. He's missing."

Tabby and Mrs. Snow light up like Christmas trees. This is probably the most intrigue either of them have seen in years. "Absolutely. I'd love to help. What happened?"

I decide to tell them part-truths, mostly so things will be easier to keep straight in my head. "Well. His girlfriend went by his place. Tried calling." I lean forward. "She thinks he's cheating."

That earns me a gasp.

"Well, I never!" Mrs. Snow puts a hand on her heart.

Tabby stands. "Let me get the ball. I'll be right back. We'll see if we can't catch this scumbag in action!" She returns a second later carrying a clear bowling-ball that should be-by the laws of physics-way too heavy for her. She plops it onto the table. "Okay. So I need a name and a little bit of a physical description."

Shit. I don't even have a last name. Hopefully what I have is enough. "Timmy. And he's a unicorn shifter."

They both turn to stare at me. "A unicorn cheating?" they

chorus, in unison. Most people think unicorns are uber-pure, just like they think nymphs are nymphomaniacs. But there's always the odd apple in any group.

I shrug. "That's what she said. But he's missing. I'm more worried about that."

Tabby nods and gets to work. Mrs. Snow slurps her tea. And I pat myself on the back. I think I'm gonna solve this whole freakish murder case before Bennett. That gives me a great deal of satisfaction.

Until I see the image Tabby pulls up in her ball. There's a unicorn-shifter, rainbow hair spread across the ground. He's laying underneath some trees. And he does not look alive.

"Oh, feculence!" I curse.

The three of us glance up at each other. We're not quite sure what to say. Or what to do.

"Should we call the police?" Mrs. Snow asks.

Tabby's head immediately sweeps side to side. Before yesterday, I wouldn't have agreed with her. But now that I've been to the dungeon, I really don't want to go back.

"I don't know…" I draw out my response, trying to figure out a logical reason for avoiding the law. The side that I'm supposed to work for. How did my life get so messed up in one night?

"First, we don't really know where he is," Tabby throws out. "Those trees could be anywhere."

"Well, we also don't know what's going on," I point out. "For all we know, he could have gone on a bender and is sleeping it off." I've never heard of a unicorn going on a bender, but you know ... it could happen. I peer closer at the crystal ball, trying to see if his horn looks shaved. I can't tell. That's when I hear something.

"What's that?" I turn to Tabby.

"Someone's coming."

Mrs. Snow looks at her front door, but Tabby pulls her back to the ball. "Not there. Here."

We all huddle over the ball. I'm surprised our breath doesn't mist the surface.

"See, someone's about to find him," I whisper to Mrs. Snow. He'll be okay.

Voices drift out of the ball as the walking noises get louder. It's clearly a couple walking in the woods.

"It's easy. I told them you were with me. You do the same," the man's voice says.

"We can't do that," the woman argues.

"We have to. There's a lot at stake. You say you were with me. Say we were looking at financials."

"But someone might have seen us. They'll know it's not true."

A foot becomes visible on the edge of the ball.

"Matt, I don't feel—" the woman's shriek has all three of us reeling back away from the ball.

"Found him," Tabby cleans out her ear. "She didn't have to be so loud about it though."

"Yes, well now we don't have to worry about calling the police," Mrs. Snow heaves a relieved sigh.

The man and woman step closer, bending to take Timmy's pulse. I knock my chair over, standing so suddenly. Tabby and Mrs. Snow both stare at me.

"Can I get my keys?" My voice is breathless. I don't have any breath. Because I can't breathe. I can barely think as Mrs. Snow hands me the keys.

"You alright sugar?" she asks.

"Sick," I mumble. I stumble out of her place and up the stairs to mine. My hands shake as I fight my lock. Once I'm inside, I sink to the floor against the door, hands covering my face.

The man and woman who found Timmy—the couple who were talking about financials—were Saffron Watts and Matthew Boolye. My mentor and that real estate mogul. In the woods together. Talking about covering for each other. Talking about alibis. They might as well have been talking about murder.

CHAPTER 11

I stare at the floor for what feels like a really long time. I'm in shock. I think it's finally hitting me that all this is real. You'd think I'd have had that realization happen in the dungeon, or the interrogation room, but no. I'm in over my head. I'm surrounded by suspects and a murderer. And I don't know what to do next. A tear slides down my cheek.

Pounding on my front door brings me back to life.

"I'm not here!" I yell.

"I have a key," Bennett's voice sounds through the door.

I groan but slide out of the way. "Why do you have a key?"

"JR gave me hers so that I could come back and do a postmortem on your 'date.'" I can hear the air quotes in his voice.

"That's it. Her friend card is totally revoked." I slide down the wall next to the door and sit on my butt as Bennett tromps in.

He glances around for second. I'm slightly amused by how lost he looks when he doesn't see me. But I ruin it by snickering. He whirls around to find me behind the door.

"What are you doing down there?"

"Giving up."

He crouches down and rubs the tear from my cheek with his thumb. For a second I see pity. But I glare at him and it quickly turns to harassment. "Giving up on what? The idiot idea you should date a criminal? The destruction of district attorney investigative property? The idea that I'm your stalker and not here to help you?"

"Were you always this annoying?" I push him away from me and stand up.

He wolf whistles. My hands immediately fly to my skirt. Dammit. It's a ridden up on my right thigh. I shove it back down.

"Stop that." I go over to the nook in the corner where my desk and computer sit. As annoying as he is, he's spurred me out of my funk. And he's right. We have to get to the bottom of things. I need to know how his investigation is going. And he needs to see what I found out. We have to figure out who the killer is. Even if Saffron's involved.

I shove that thought away.

I flip on the computer and pull the spy camera out of my hair.

Bennett flops onto the couch irritated. He pulls out a notebook. "I need to know what happened after you pulled that childish little act in the bathroom Ly-ly. Luke is my prime suspect. What did he say?"

"He shouldn't be your prime suspect."

I boot up the video program.

"Hey! Pay attention please." Ben crosses and puts his hand on my shoulder. I shrug him off and sync the camera's bluetooth with the computer.

"Ly, this is a serious investigation."

"I know," I turn and grab his shoulders. Damn. He's more ripped than when we dated. He could maybe give Luke a run for his money. Not that I'm comparing. I would never. I'm over him. I force him into my computer chair. I press play. "I recorded my entire night. You're gonna want to watch everything."

"Everything?" his eyes flick to mine. "You don't mean anything happened …"

I roll my eyes. "Nothing like that. Just watch. The suspect list is worse than you ever thought."

"What's that mean?"

I refuse to answer and point to the screen. He turns and starts watching.

I walk to the kitchen. I just ate but all this detective work, lying, and craziness is stressing me out. It's time for ice cream. I grab a pint of bubblegum for myself and some caramel for Bennett. I bring his to him and collapse onto the couch with mine.

I MUST HAVE FALLEN ASLEEP, BECAUSE THE NEXT THING I know, Bennett is shaking me awake.

"Hey," his breath on my ear is soft and sweet. It brings up memories. I turn toward him, my hands reaching out. I caress his stubble.

I realize what I'm doing. I jolt backward on the couch. "Sorry. Um. Sorry."

He smiles softly. A little sadly maybe. But I'm really not awake, so how am I supposed to tell?

"I watched everything."

I nod, rubbing my eyes, scooting over on the couch so he can sit. I feel my cheek, the velvet pattern of the couch has left squiggle marks all over it. Gorgeous. Great.

"Nice work with the spy cam. What made you think of that?"

"Runes. His tattoos could have anti-spy spell runes in them."
I think back to my cellmate and his advice on runes. I
wonder if Luke would let me photograph his tattoos with an
infrared camera. The idea of him taking off his shirt and
letting me take photos momentarily sidetracks me. Why did
I turn him down again? Oh right. Murder investigation.
Suspect. Focus.

Bennett grins. "I think you might need some caffeine. I'll
make coffee."

I blush as he leaves. I'm so, so glad he cannot read my dirty
mind. I decide I need to move a bit to wake up more, so I
stand. "What time is it?"

"Four a.m."

I stretch. When I head toward the kitchen, Bennett's
standing frozen, his hands on the coffee bag, staring at me.

I give him a quizzical look. He snaps out of it and hastily
starts pouring coffee into the machine. "You did good work,"
he mutters. "There are a lotta people with a lot of reasons to
hate Georgina right now."

"I know. I hope if I'm ever murdered, it's not this hard to
solve." I hop up onto the counter before I remember I'm in a
short skirt.

Bennett's dazed look returns and I get an inkling about why he froze before.

I snap in his face as I adjust my skirt. "Excuse me, *co-worker*. We were starting a conversation about suspects."

He turns bright red. Ha. So I was right. He was gawking.

He fumbles with my cabinets, searching for coffee cups. I could help him out, but I decide I'm enjoying his discomfort too much.

"So, I showed you mine. Your turn."

He whips around when I say that, eyes wide. I can see a flash of heat in them before he gasps, "What?" I bet if I touched his skin right now, he'd be blazing hot.

"What evidence have you picked up so far? Who've you interviewed? What's the working theory?"

He takes a deep breath to calm himself before he responds.

"I've talked to her parents. And I'm not supposed to discuss the case with a suspect."

I roll my eyes. "I'm not really a suspect."

He shrugs. "You knew her."

"More like knew of her. It's not like she hung out with high school kids when I dated …" It's hard for me to say Alec's name, even now. I don't know at this point if it's because I kept him a secret so long, or if it's just always hard to think of your first heartbreak.

"The parents are weird." Bennett caves. I'm not sure why, exactly. But I do his silence thing. That tactic that lets the silence stretch out until the weaker person has to fill it. And he does. "The mom, I dunno if she drank someone who was high or what, but she kept dodging questions. 'I'm not sure.' 'I don't remember exactly.' 'Are we done?'" He mocks her in a falsetto that would make any choir boy proud.

I frown. "I don't remember her being a ditz."

"She's not. She's an engineer. Socially awkward I'd get, but it was like she couldn't remember-"

I interject. "Like maybe she'd been given something to forget? Like maybe unicorn horn?"

Bennett pours our coffees and sweetens mine. "That's what I was thinking, yeah."

"So, someone killed Georgina and erased her mom's memory. Is there an antidote for unicorn horn?"

"Nope. Not that I've found. It's crazy hard to get, since unicorns are so protective of their magic."

I shake my head at him. "I'm disappointed. There was totally opportunity for a dirty joke there. And you dodged it."

"Well, *co-worker*," Bennett snipes back. "I'm trying to keep this conversation focused."

"On long pointed objects that can make women forget their own name?"

He sighs. "Do you want me to tell you any more or are you gonna keep doing that?"

"Doing what?" I bat my eyes. Bennett tosses a dishrag at my face.

"Mr. Knight was monosyllabic. Yes, no answers only. Also suspicious. You know what else? They're making us get a search warrant to get into Georgina's apartment. They wouldn't just let us in. Why wouldn't parents want to help us find their daughter's killer?" He hands me a steaming coffee mug.

I take a sip of perfectly-made, sweet coffee. "You know why. Because they might be helping her killer."

"They might be the killers themselves."

I sigh and raise a hand to my forehead ala Southern damsel in distress. "Why Bennett, whatever will we do? Our list of suspects is a mile long. Everyone who knew Georgina wanted to kill her. Maybe we should just let bygones be bygones."

Bennett growls at that. It's a hot sound, and my eyes meet his. For a moment, attraction flares in both our eyes.

He turns away first. And I'm hit by a sharp pang of rejection. But I shouldn't be, right? I shouldn't care at all. Because I have a hot-as-sin vamp that I started seeing (and hope to keep seeing if he is not-after-all a murderer). And it's been years. I should have better armor than this. I play it off like it didn't happen.

"So, what next?" I go for casual, taking another sip of coffee.

"I want you to stay at my place." Bennett's response has me spraying coffee across the room.

"What?"

Calmly, he picks up the dishrag and wipes his face as though it's no big deal he just got hit with molten sugar water. "You lost your keys, right?"

"What else is new?"

He narrows his eyes. "You've never lost your keys on a date with a known gangster before, Lyon. Luke Hawkins is under suspicion for trafficking, gambling, money laundering, and a whole list of things I don't even want to say."

I narrow my eyes in response. "One, I lose my keys at least once a day. Two, if he's suspected of those things but hasn't been arrested, it's because you have no evidence."

Bennett's growl is back. "You're gonna write it off because we can't prove it yet? Or because you're hot for him? Tell me, does that make sense, Ly-ly?" He's angry, and steps forward, forcing me to look up at him.

Oh man. So ninety percent of the time, the dominance thing

just pisses me off. But when a guy is all worked up over your safety... whew, call the fire department. Because I think my panties just spontaneously combusted. I can't help myself. I have to ask, "Why do you care, Bennett?"

A look I can't read passes over his face. He doesn't answer but puts a hand on my arm. It's blazing hot. Which means he's just as worked up as I am. "Pack your bags. Now."

And I do. Because if there will ever be a repeat of that moment, where his finger leaves a gentle trail of fire down my arm, it'll be worth another breakup. Seriously. I almost orgasmed right then.

That leaves my thoughts buzzing like idiot flies in my head. They say things like, 'Wow, murder is cool.' And 'If the end result is two hot guys, maybe you should get arrested more often.' I decide I need my coffee to go since my brain is spewing such nonsense. I drop my bags in the kitchen and grab a travel mug when two arms circle my waist.

"No time."

"What?" I try not to go weak at the knees. Which is very hard.

"Luke Hawkins is on the sidewalk out front. We're going out the balcony."

I freeze. "He's here to break into my place?"

"I set up your spy-cam again. If he does, we'll figure out exactly what he wants."

With that, Bennett scoops me into his arms. He grabs my travel bag and tosses it onto my lap. He throws open my rear balcony doors. And then, in full sight of Tabby and Mrs. Snow, who are walking across the lawn below, he shifts.

His clothes shred as his skin turns into black scales lined with red, and as his face morphs into a fierce fire-breathing dragon. I feel the changes because he keeps me pressed against his hard chest the entire time. Mmm... I can see why Mrs. Snow and Tabby love to watch. But being right next to the action, caught up in the magical vortex of his change. It's indescribable. I don't have time to describe it anyway, because a second after he's done shifting, Bennett spreads his wings and we're off.

CHAPTER 12

Being swept away to Bennett's place is not at all like the romantic getaway I first pictured when he said he wanted me to stay with him. First of all, flying in a dragon's claws is an experience I do not recommend. Even though he's cradling me like a baby, his claws are sharp. Super ouch.

Second, I realize Bennett's not taking me to his stone cottage near the caves. He's bringing me somewhere I've never been before.

Apparently, Bennett now lives in a brownstone town home better suited for the East Coast than the California sunshine. It's part of Fire Row, an old housing development for dragons. A lot of the more ancient dragons and the New Age dragons prefer the caves back in the hills. Most dragon clans, including Ben's, talk up the 'traditional life.'

It's only the more type-A businessy dragons like Bennett that live here. Hence the unkempt lawns. I mean, really, who works and has still has time to mow? I get it. But the overgrown shrubs make the block look haunted, not welcoming, in the pre-dawn light.

"Well this is ... scenic." I comment sarcastically. I turn and look up at him. "I didn't think you'd ever leave that cottage. I thought you liked it there." It had never been my favorite, all his family members just dropping by without an invite, but Bennett had loved being surrounded by them. I'm surprised by the move. Makes me wonder what his new place is like.

Bennett lands on the roof, shifts, and brings me down a set of stairs. His door opens after he speaks a password in Drakon, the dragon language.

He helps, a.k.a. shoves, me inside in front of him. Apparently, I don't walk fast enough for him. Can a girl help it if a naked guy with a six pack is a distraction? I swear I didn't look on purpose. (Not like it's anything I haven't seen before anyway.) But I'm trying to maintain some kind of professionalism here. Unlike Mr. Shovey-hands.

I roll my eyes once we're in his living/kitchen area, pull out a kitchen chair, and stare pointedly at the wall as he walks to his room to change.

I hear a bleating and turn to see a lamb tied to a ring in the corner of the kitchen. Floor to ceiling around the lamb is stone, scorched black. I'd better not be here through dinner. That's all I know.

I pat Lambie on the head and decide to wander to the couch instead of further befriending Bennett's future meal.

The living room is a typical bachelor pad. Functional. Utilitarian. Black furniture. Beige walls and carpet. Boring.

The move didn't lead to a major revelation on the decoration front. I wonder if Bennett's having issues with his mom. He was always a momma's boy. But … not my place. I'm here for work and safety reasons only.

I call out to Bennett, "So what's our next move?"

He comes back in khakis and a T-shirt. "Sorry slugger," he ruffles my hair like he's some annoying big brother. "You're gonna have to sit this one out."

He did not just say that! After all that evidence I just got him?

"I just got you like one million pieces of evidence."

Bennett smiles. "Yes, but you're not an investigator."

My fury has no words.

Bennett revels for a second. Then he takes pity on me. "Look. My next move is to go talk to Saffron. Clearly she's hiding something."

"It was Matthew Boolye who wanted to hide something. Saffron told him no!"

"Which is why I'm going to talk to her first. She might still be feeling honest enough to come clean." He grabs the keys to his front door. "You can order in." He slides a credit card onto the kitchen counter. He chucks me across the chin and then heads to the door.

"I'm ordering a stripper!"

"As long as it's a girl!" He yells back as he shuts and locks the door behind him.

Gah!

I cannot stand that man. Even if his naked ass is so hot it could fry pancakes.

I pull out my cell and call JR.

I don't even greet her when she answers. I'm too desperate. "Girl time, stat."

It's late enough that she can slip out of the office unnoticed. I hope.

She breathes a sigh of relief. "Oh good. I was gonna call you. I got the worst news."

"Did you get arrested for murder too?"

"What? No."

"Then it can wait. Get your butt over to Bennett's house and then we can talk."

"Wait. What are you doing at Bennett's?"

I hang up instead of answering her. I figure if nothing else, that will get Ms. Goody-good to leave the office. I text her my phone's location. Then I use my phone to search the menu of the priciest delivery place in town.

TWO DELICIOUS BROWN-SUGAR RIB-EYE STEAKS LATER, JR AND I are sprawled across Bennett's crappy 'mod' couch drinking his booze. Typical dragon, he didn't have any sweet mix-ins, so I've stolen all the sugar packets from his coffee stash to make simple syrup. JR raided the fridge for limes. We're drinking gimlets. I've added extra sugar to my drink, because gin, really Bennett? You might as well have me lick a metal pole.

JR's eyelids droop. She's listened to me rehash my entire night.

"Is it my turn yet?" she asks with a yawn.

"Oh. Yeah. Sorry. Go for it."

"You are hereby required to go to dinner with me tomorrow night."

I raise my brows. "Okay. But I thought you said you had bad news."

"You are required to go to dinner with me and Liam tomorrow night."

I groan. JR's little brother Liam is a first-rate jerk. I mean bad. He's the VP at some sporting goods business in Thousand Oaks. He lives among humans, so he thinks he's the shit. Obviously, the nymph gene helps with that. It also means he prides himself on being a "catch" as though he's done something to deserve that title. Ick. Plus a goatee. I mean really. How much more stuck in the 90's can you get? Worst, he's always getting on JR's case about her ambition. Paralegal isn't good enough. Not a career path.

"Basically, you're telling me I need to get drunk before dinner."

She nods. "Danny has a soccer game so he won't be able to go. There will be no buffer." Danny is her satyr boyfriend. He's on a rec-league soccer team. Think about it, a soccer team made of half-goat men? How much attention does the ball get versus the grass? I totally think it's an excuse for a guy's night out chewing the cud.

Danny is one of the world's nicest guys. So, he typically can keep up a conversation and prevent Liam from constantly nitpicking JR to death. I, on the other hand, have been known to get in shouting matches with Liam. Tomorrow night's gonna be a blast.

I toss my head back in a pout. "Maybe I'll punish Bennett and make him come with me."

JR raises an eyebrow. "Like a date?"

"No. Like a punishment for leaving me here."

"You know when you get bossy with boys you're actually flirting, right?"

I throw a pillow at her.

"Are you into Bennett?"

"No!" She does not look like she believes my totally authentic but totally drunken denial. It's not my fault it came out slurred. It's the gimlets. They're messing with my tongue. "I don't repeat my mistakes."

"Maybe you guys weren't a mistake. Maybe you were just too young," She yawns and ignores the second pillow that misses her by a mile.

"I'm not too young. And give me back my pillow!"

She laughs and shakes her head. "Well, I'm definitely not young anymore. I'm exhausted. This old lady's got to fly." She grabs her phone to get a Broomer.

She ignores my hand flailing through the air, trying to catch a pillow she most definitely hasn't—but should have—thrown to me.

"Night, Ly-ly. Enjoy dreaming about Bennett and your hot vamp."

My best friend leaves me drunk and helpless, in the

apartment of a fire-breathing dragon man who once scorched my heart. I plot vengeance for a minute before I drift into a dreamless nap.

WHEN I WAKE UP HALF AN HOUR LATER, BENNETT'S STILL NOT back. I decide he needs a little bit more punishment for not taking me with him. His couch sucks. My neck has a crick in it. I decide he can take the couch and I'll take the master bed. I grab my overnight bag and go into his room, locking the door behind me.

I turn around and drop my bag on my foot. "Mother duckling!" That would be my curling iron. Curse my vanity. Damn.

I kick the bag away to punish it and take a step closer to his bed. There, above the headboard, is a photo I took three years ago. He's blown it up on a canvas print. It's a beautiful picture, one I'm really proud of. A fairy child was kidnapped several years back, and I was part of the search team. Everybody had mocked me for bringing my camera along like a nerd, but I'd brought my zoom lens. I'd kept the camera trained on the ground as we combed the forest for the kid. If I hadn't, we never would've seen that delicate little wingtip. It had ripped on a broken tree branch and dangled like a spider web. It was so little. So tiny. I might not have recognized it if I hadn't had a wing obsession growing up.

(Imagine that. A wingless fairy with a wing obsession. How stereotypically female of me.)

That picture helped us narrow the search. It helped us find the little girl. That picture represents one of the best moments of my life.

Why does Bennett have it blown up over his bed?

Is he sentimental? About the search? About me? Or is it only my ego that wants it to be about me?

Do I ask him about this? Is this something we should talk about? Or would that up the awkward factor even more?

I wish JR hadn't gone home.

I trash the punishment plan and shower and change. I return to the couch. I wait and wait. But Bennett doesn't come home. At least not before I drift off to sleep. Fairy wings and fruit tarts and hot tattooed vampires fill my dreams. I'm about to lick some delicious whipped cream off a bicep when my phone rings.

I fall off the couch.

"Darn it!"

I search, bleary-eyed for my phone. It's got to be almost 4:00 p.m. Who the heck is calling me? I find the phone and answer.

"Hello?"

"Honey, I need your help." Jacob's voice is desperate. It sounds like he's been crying. Immediately, I sit up.

"What is it?"

"It's Saffron. I think—I think she might have had something to do with Georgina's death."

CHAPTER 13

I drop the phone and it slides under the couch. I reach into the gap to grab it but it's just past my reach. I have to get full-body on the floor. I flail my arm around and feel my fingers touch the very edge of the phone.

"Hold on Jacob," I call as I go around to the back side of the couch. I get on my knees and shove my hand back under the gap.

Of course, I don't hear Bennett come in. I'm too focused on clutching my phone and trying to extricate my hand from under the sofa.

"This is the second time in two days I've found you crawling around on the floor. Is this some kind of new thing with you?" Bennett's eyes are joking.

I don't have time for jokes right now. Not after what Jacob just told me. I pull the phone up and back to my ear. I wave Bennett off.

He rolls his eyes and saunters toward his bedroom.

"Jacob?" I whisper, creeping across the living room. I pull open the front door and step outside. I do not want Bennett overhearing this conversation.

"Are you okay?"

"Yes. Sorry. Dropped the phone." Normally this would have earned me a chuckle. Not now. "I missed everything after you said Saffron might … you know …" I can't even say the words. It feels like sacrilege.

"You know the quilts we gave her?" Jacob asks.

"Yeah?"

"It's not a joke anymore. She hardly ever sleeps at home. Sometimes I don't see her for two days straight."

I have to force myself to hold onto the phone this time. "Has she had a lot of trials lately?"

"No."

"What about campaign stuff?"

"No."

I take a deep breath. The next question is hard. "Are you guys having … problems?"

Jacob's sigh turns into a sob. "I'm not sure."

"I'm on my way over."

I slip back inside to grab a few things only to find Bennett right inside the door.

"Eavesdropper."

"Investigator," he counters. "Was that Jacob Watts?"

I squint up at him. "Am I allowed to talk to him?"

He gives a shrug. "I wouldn't mind if you'd wear another spelled recorder."

"Around Jacob? Are you kidding?" I push him.

"I'm not. Ly, I had to wait around Saffron's chambers to pull her in for a second interview. And who walked out of chambers with her?"

"Who?" My chest gets tight.

"Matthew Boolye. I'll give you two guesses how my interview went."

"She lied?" Oh shit. Oh shit. No. Saffron's always been … determined, logical. Calculating. Cold. Some people think she's cold. I blink up at Bennett.

"She lied. Said she and Matthew were going over financials when Georgina was murdered. You know what the video monitors at Abra Casino show? Both of them leaving the meeting room after the confrontation with Georgina. They walk down the hall. But strangely enough, the camera around the corner wasn't working. I have a witch and and an IT guy on it, but ..."

"But. But ..." I have no clue what to say. "What about the unicorn guy? Did they report him?"

"Matthew did. No mention of Saffron. The unicorn himself just remembers Georgina. No one else."

I sit straight down. On the floor. My world is spinning. "She didn't report it." She's always been upstanding. She's always been my apple-pie-in-the-sky bad-ass, kick-ass hero. She's a judge. She has to report stuff like that. A sinking part of me wonders how right Jacob is. Is the Saffron I knew and loved gone?

Bennett crouches next to me. He rubs my shoulder.

"I have to go see Jacob. I told him I was going."

Bennett nods, then stands and jogs over to his desk. He pulls out an ugly-as-crap spelled bracelet. This one has a bottle cap instead of a coin as a trinket. Whoever supplies the investigation team has terrible taste. He wraps the chain twice around my wrist and fastens it.

"Why do you keep making me do this?" My eyes fill with tears.

"I'm not the only investigator on this, Ly." Bennett clears his throat.

"What's that supposed to mean?"

"It means I might not think you did it. And we might have some evidence to the contrary. But her parents won't confirm your humanizing theory. They won't confirm anything really. And there's nobody else in town who can confirm what you say about your blood. No legal way for me to do it. But the more you go out of your way to help as an informant ..."

"Who thinks I did it?"

He shrugs. I want to punch him and make him tell me.

"It's someone who's friends with Arnold isn't it?" That pudgy ass!

He shrugs again. I know it has to be. Arnold and I have a staunch mutual-hate relationship. Even so, it hurts a little. But thinking about that's not gonna do any good. Right now, I wish I was a witch. That I had enough magic to turn back time and undo it all. But wishes won't get me anywhere. Instead, I have a scratchy spelled bracelet.

I rub at my eyes, exhaustion creeping back over me. It's only been a few days. But the stress has made it feel endless.

"What do I say?" I picture Jacob, my poor sweet coyote man.

If he hasn't shifted and started howling out his cries by the time I get there, I'll be surprised.

"Just listen."

"Great advice. On the suck-o-meter that's a whopping 9.5. Just listen?" I wish I had packed a camera. That spy-cam worked out so well last time.

Bennett sighs. "You better get going."

"I need a key."

"Why? You'll just lose it."

I punch his arm. But Bennett does not get up to give me a key. "I'll be here when you get back. Probably. If not, I can fly back in like five minutes."

Fine. He wants to be that way about my shortcomings. "Sure. Five minutes. Except if it's like that one time—"

His eyes flare. "Do not."

"Oh, I will. Took you almost half an hour to get home. I sat on the steps. My butt was numb."

"It wasn't my fault," he grits his teeth.

"I told you not to eat nine chili dogs."

"Just go." He pushes me toward the door and outside.

I turn. He slams the door in my face, hoping to end the conversation.

But I'm not down with that. "Had to land every two minutes to find a bush!" I yell. "Remember that? Squirts?!" I yell the nickname his friends and I gave him after that incident. Took him months to live it down. Am I petty? Yup. But, come on. He dragged me to his apartment, forced me to stay behind during his investigation, told me some people still think I'm a murderer, and then kicked me out without a key.

Bennett doesn't respond. I go to kick his door but it flies open, making me fall flat on my butt. *Smack!* Mother eff!

He glares down at me. His green stare is intense. "You want to resurrect old nicknames, Orphan?"

Low blow. Bringing up my mom issues is not cool.

"Just give me a key."

"No."

"Why? And don't tell me it's because I lose them."

"I don't ..." he pauses and his eyes flicker inside.

"You don't want me in there without you. Why? Girlfriend?"

"No."

"But you left me there once without you already."

His neck starts to get red.

"Is this about the photo?"

139

The heat creeps up his cheeks. Embarrassment washes over his face.

"I've seen it. In large living color."

"Why were you in my bedroom?"

I shrug. "I was gonna kick you to the couch."

He shakes his head. "Ly. I wanted to talk before—"

"Before I saw it?"

He sighs and nods. He offers me a hand up from the ground. His hand is warm and hard and latches onto mine. I stare at our hands for a moment and things get entirely too serious. I can't handle it.

"Took you long enough to remember to be a gentleman," I scoff. "But, I guess stalkers aren't used to being gentlemen."

"Not a stalker."

I roll my eyes and pull my hand gently away. "Yeah. Sure, French. Not a stalker." I'm not ready to deal with the serious look in his eyes. I twirl and run down the steps. I pause at the bottom to summon a Broomer. Within a minute, a witch appears, hovering in mid-air in front of me. I peek back up at Bennett. He hasn't left the stoop.

I hop on the Broomer. As the witch wheels around I yell, "I've counted my underwear. It better all still be there when I get back!"

SAFFRON AND JACOB LIVE IN THE CLIFFS. IT'S A GATED
community. And the name is literal. As in each house is at
the top of a small man-made cliff. Great for thunderbirds
who fly like Saffron. Why Jacob agreed to it, I don't know.
He's always been the giver. Man, I hope he's just stressed. I
hope he's wrong. I hope Saffron hasn't nose-dived from the
pressure of the campaign.

But Georgina went crazy. I mean, she attacked me that night.
She hardly knows me. Probably doesn't even know my last
name. And Georgina just owns a vamp B&B (Bed and Blood).
She didn't have near the stress level Saffron does. I mean,
Saffron locks creatures away. She works death penalty cases.
That's gotta take a toll. Has she had a breakdown?

I think about her behavior. Run through my memories. She
was a little late to my birthday dinner. But when is she not
running late? I haven't noticed her be weird around Jacob.
Maybe ... maybe quieter. But you know, people mellow in
their old age. Ben's news and Jacob's call shake me.

The witch flies me to the Watts' doorstep. I don't even have
to ring the bell. Jacob's there. He's not sobbing but his eyes
are red.

"Come in."

Jacob paces while I sit on the leather couch. It's like he
doesn't know what to do with himself. Honestly, it's a little

scary to watch your rock melt down. I mean, Jacob's been there for me for almost a decade. Since my dad passed. And I've never seen him like this. He wrings his hands. His eyes fill up with tears.

I open my arms. He sits next to me. I let him cry on my shoulder. Every so often, his breathing hitches. He calms himself to quiet. But then a thought will set him off again. We're on the couch until it's nearly sunset.

When he's finally cried out, I turn to him. "Tell me."

"Judge Gruff. She was on the phone with Gruff," Jacob begins.

Gruff's another felony judge. Head of the unit. He's the one who assigns judges to different courtrooms. He's also the judge that signs off on search warrants.

"She asked Gruff to wait on the warrant for Georgina."

I gasp. Search warrants are the legal way for our investigators to get into private property and get evidence. Interfering is a big no no. It can tarnish a case. Evidence can get lost. Hidden. Erased. My eyes meet Jacob's. He stops walking, as though telling me has emptied him of nervous energy. Getting the truth out has drained him.

"Does she know you heard?"

He nods slowly. "She had the door cracked. Pacing while she talked. She turned. Saw me."

"What did she say?"

"After she hung up, she told me she was trying to protect you."

My heart cracks just a little. "She thinks I did it?"

Jacob crosses the room and crouches in front of me in time to swipe away a tear from my cheek. "No, honey. I don't really think she does. I know I don't. But the only reason I can see her doing that ..."

"Is if there's something at Georgina's apartment she doesn't want everyone to see."

He nods. "That night, Georgina didn't just threaten you, sweet pea. She threatened Saffron."

He's right. She did. Georgina had been spewing all kinds of threats. I kinda only focused on mine once her hands were around my neck. I feel like puking. Jacob's information, combined with Bennett's information earlier about the hall cameras ... I have to swallow the bile. I can't break down in front of Jacob. "But what could she have known about Saffron?"

Jacob shakes his head. "I'm not sure. That's what I want you to come with me to find out."

I nod. "Where are we going?"

"Where else? Georgina's apartment."

One spelled tablet and a hair-raising cliff-ride later, I'm ducking through alleyways on Jacob's back, second-guessing my sanity. Not just my wisdom. I definitely should have said no. This is a stupid idea. I have no wisdom left. But did I also lose my sense of self-preservation? I just agreed to a B&E (breaking and entering—yeah, that acronym's the same) in a recorded conversation. I kind of think I might deserve lock-up, just not the kind Arnold and friends want for me. The padded cell kind.

When Jacob gets close to Georgina's apartment, he stops. I slide off, my legs still trembling with adrenaline. Jacob hides behind a dumpster to shift and change. I fumble in my pocket for a spelled tablet to get bigger, but a hand stops me.

"Don't," Jacob's eyes pierce mine as he crouches to reach my mini-me eye-level. "You'll be less noticeable if you stay small." It's just after sunset, and everything is that hazy shade of grey. He's right. If I stay small, I'll be able to watch more.

"What about you? You might have been able to pass for a dog. Someone might recognize you."

He shrugs away the danger. "I need my hands."

My hands start to shake. How can he be so nonchalant about this? "Are you sure this is a good idea? I mean. At the very least it's trespassing. And it could be—"

"Lyon." He puts a hand on my shoulder. "You're not going in. And you're not keeping watch."

"But, but isn't it conspiracy if I know about the crime?"

He raises his eyebrows. "What crime? I'm gonna go upstairs and knock on the door. Georgina's father's supposedly been staying at her place to keep investigators out until he verifies they've got a warrant. I'm just gonna go in and talk to him. Maybe take an extended trip to the bathroom." He winks.

"Oh. Oh." I put a hand over my heart, forcing it to calm down. "You coulda' told me that before we left. I've been freaking out this whole ride."

"Sorry. I would never do that to you, you know."

I shake my head. "I know. I just. These past few nights have been hard."

Jacob scoops me up into a massive hug. And being the size of a two-year old, I get the amazing sensation of safety and comfort. It reminds me of being a little kid. I don't want to let go.

A clanging noise jolts us apart. At first I think someone's thrown something at the dumpster behind us. But then Jacob points up. A man in a mask hurries down the fire escape above us. Out a window on the third floor.

"Didn't you say Georgina's apartment was on the third floor?" I turn to Jacob. I have a bad feeling about this.

He nods. "Get out of here and call the cops." He takes off toward the fire escape.

I start down the alley but turn when I smell smoke. My eyes flicker upward.

Georgina's apartment is on fire.

CHAPTER 14

"**F**ire!" I yell. Fire. Shit. Shit. Oh shit. Where's my phone? I search my pockets frantically, so I can call this in. I don't feel my phone. "Son of a Trucker! I must have left my phone at Jacob's." I look around, ready to assault a stranger for a good cause. But nobody's around this time of night. Except there, rounding the corner away from me.

"Stop!" I sprint toward the stranger. "There's a fire! We need to call the cops! Stop!" I barrel right into the man's back. I latch onto his trench coat to keep from falling face first into the pavement. I've had enough head injuries for one week, thank you. I let go as soon as I'm sure I've got my balance. "Sorry." I realize that I would probably be better off normal-sized. The man might have heard me better. I take the spelled tablet to get big again.

The man turns. I gasp.

"Luke?!"

He holds a box in his hands. A box of belongings that looks suspiciously like a break-up box. My eyes flicker from the box back up to him.

"What are you doing here?" he asks.

I shake my head. "In a sec. Georgina's apartment is on fire. I can't find my phone. I need yours!"

His eyes snap over to the building and widen. I can't tell if it's real or faux surprise. A shiver of fear runs through me. Did I just run into the arsonist?

"Shit!" Luke curses and shoves the box at me. A phone lands on top of the pile. "Georgina's dad's in there!" He sprints back toward the brick apartment complex, where flames now lick the top floor windows. Residents from the lower floors are streaming out. Someone must have warned them.

Guilt washes over me as I watch Luke yank open the front door and push his way inside, toward danger. Toward one of the few things that can kill a vampire. Fire. How could I have misjudged him like that? I kick myself. I drop his box at my feet and grab the phone, dialing 9-1-1.

The cops roll up as I'm giving details to the dispatcher. "Never mind. Looks like cops are here. Just make sure fire's on the way." I hang up. I'm about to wade through the crowd to tell the police to send a man inside to look for Luke when he comes stumbling out. He's covered in soot. And he's alone. I start toward him, but the cops swarm him like little blue bees.

They cuff him before I can take more than three steps. I'm about to stomp on over and scream at them in public—not my best idea, admittedly—but a hand on my shoulder stops me.

"Don't. We'll sort it out down at the station." Bennett orders.

"But he just went in there to try to save Mr. Knight."

Ben nods, eyes taking in the scene. "I know. I heard. Remember?" He gestures toward the spelled bottle cap bracelet. "I called dispatch when you couldn't find your phone." He eyes the fire, which suddenly roars as it finds new fuel.

"Don't tell me you're gonna go in there!" My chest tightens at the thought, even though my brain tells me to shut it. As a dragon, Ben's practically fireproof. If someone could get Mr. Knight out, it would be him.

"Can't. Don't have jurisdiction. Plus, we don't know what caused the fire. If it's magical, I can't withstand it."

"But we can't let them arrest Luke!" I feel panic and indignation at the same time.

"The crowd gets closure. The cops look like good guys.

Hawkins gets a bad half-hour maybe, but you and I will follow the squad car and get him out. Where's Jacob?"

I turn, searching the crowd. "I dunno." I'd forgotten about him. "He was in the alley on the side of the building. We saw someone climbing down the fire escape from Georgina's ..." Crap. That was probably the real arsonist. And I'd left sixty-three-year-old Jacob chasing after a criminal by himself. I hope he shifted to coyote form to chase that shit-head. I snatch up Luke's box and follow Bennett toward the alley.

"Stay back, Lyon. You don't know what's down there."

"If Jacob's hurt, I want to help."

Bennett rounds on me at the mouth of the alley. "Stay put. You may be my informant, but you are not an investigator. If that guy's still around—" He doesn't get to finish his lecture.

At that moment a very naked Jacob comes trudging down the alley, holding his hand to a nasty gash on his head. I flip around quickly and let Bennett get the clothes issue sorted. The firefighters have arrived and they are moving the crowd to make room for their equipment. A cop runs over and lets them know someone is still inside. Or so I assume, from the fact that three of them grab axes, pull down their masks, and trudge under the column of smoke to the door of the building.

A Channel Thirteen van pulls up and a hair-sprayed brunette nymph hops out. Her camera man follows and she starts spouting off to the camera. How she knows what to say, I don't know. It's not like she consulted the cops.

The camera glints in the fire. I wonder if they're standing too close to the heat. Heat. Camera.

I turn back around, grateful that Jacob's now decent. "Ben, you need to get the cops to take infrared pictures."

"What?" He's busy taking Jacob's statement about the man on the fire escape. He chased the man but the suspect threw a spelled knife that flew through the air like a missile, latching onto Jacob's face and chasing him away.

"Can we do statements back at the station? You really need to get a cop to take infrared pics of Georgina's apartment."

"There won't be anything left." Bennett eyes the extension ladder the firefighters are using to spray the top floor.

"If she had any protective runes up, they'll show," I retort.

"How do you know that?"

"A firebug told me."

"What?"

"Just do it." I tug his sleeve. "And we all need to get back to the station." I watch a police car pull away with Luke inside. "It's not fair to let them harass Luke for this."

Bennett sighs. But he complies. I see him go over to the boys in blue and chat. I look up at Jacob. "You okay?"

Jacob shakes his head no. "But this isn't why."

He's still upset about his suspicions about Saffron. And now it looks like we might never know if she was really involved or not. Did someone set the fire to get rid of evidence connected to Georgina's murder? Since the cops never got a look inside it seems likely. But was it Saffron? Or someone she hired? It looked like a man on the fire escape. Who could have done this?

"Excuse me," a bubbly voice makes me turn.

The news reporter nymph (who has readjusted her cleavage so it's very prominent) winks at me. "I'm Jackie Hanna." Her smile's as bright as the fire. Unlike the fire, which is very real, it's very very fake. Ugh. "I hear you were one of the first people to call in the fire." How does she know this? Does the station have video spells on all the street corners?

"Just doing what anyone would."

"I heard you spoke to that man who attempted a rescue." She bats her eyelashes for the camera. Gag me with a spoon. Who could stand to watch this girl? I mean, the way stupid oozes off her ... I bet she reads coloring books.

"Yes." I smile at the camera but don't give her anything else. Until a thought pops into my head. And suddenly, talking to stupid Jackie is so much more appealing. Georgina accused Saffron of spreading rumors about her to Channel Thirteen.

"Luke used to date a girl who lived in that apartment," I lean in, as if I'm confiding something. She probably already knows all this, but it'll make for decent T.V. "He was getting a box of his stuff. Her dad was still in the apartment when the fire broke out."

"Oh my gosh!" Jackie gasps. "Did Luke get her father out?"

I shake my head. "He tried. But I don't think so. A couple fireman ran in after he'd come out. They aren't back yet."

Her eyes glitter. I've just made her night. This story is now more than a house fire. It's a search and rescue with an outcome still pending. In other words, news-worthy gold.

She turns to the camera. "You heard it first here, folks. There's a man trapped inside that fire. Rescue workers are on the case. Only time will tell if this night ends in triumph or tragedy. We will keep you posted as this situation develops further. Jackie Hanna. Channel Thirteen."

The camera's light stops blinking.

Jackie turns to me and grabs my arm like we're BFF. "Thanks so much!"

"No problem. It's totally scary, what's going on." I communicate on her level. I hope it will make her feel like we're bonding. Encourage her to share a little. Though gossip is basically her business.

Jacob is looking at me oddly, so I link arms with Jackie and turn away from him. "So, I heard that vampire whose apartment caught fire—Gina or something—was the one that was murdered." I act like I didn't know that in the first place.

Jackie nods, leaning in. "Yeah. Georgina Knight. Apparently, everybody's freaked out about that. I mean, the last vamp murder in Tres Lunas was like three years ago. Or at least, the last reported one."

I bat my eyes. "Scary, right? I mean who could do that?"

"I know. Vamps are so fast."

"I heard though, that Georgina was accused of some nasty stuff before someone took her out."

Jackie nods. "Yeah. We even had some old lady come by the station and accuse her of draining."

I gasp. "No way."

"Yup."

"Is it true?"

"Well, the neighbors over there said they heard weird noises in her apartment. Yelling. Clanking. Banging. They complained to management." She jerks her head to a couple of gremlins in the crowd. "But she bit it before we could really investig—a fireman is back! Hugh!" She drops my arm and waves her camera man forward. They plow through the crowd toward a fireman emerging from the building.

So, there was something strange going on at Georgina's apartment. I add together the few facts I have uncovered. Cherry said Georgina stopped hosting parties a couple months ago. The neighbors heard weird noises. I mean, I guess her apartment could have been haunted. But that doesn't explain the draining accusation. Was Georgina keeping humans locked up in her apartment, so she could suck the life out of them? Literally?

I stare up at the flames, which are dying. The firefighters are winning the battle. But any evidence probably burned up tonight.

Whatever was hidden in that apartment, it was clear someone didn't want it discovered. Georgina was involved in something shady. And she obviously wasn't working alone. The question is, what exactly was she involved in? Who with? And was that the reason she was killed?

All I have now are questions. I see Ben making his way back to Jacob and me. Hopefully, at the station, we'll find some answers.

CHAPTER 15

Dawn's creeping over the horizon when Ben drives us to the station and pulls into the parking garage. I've never been in a police vehicle (unless someone tossed me unconscious into one after the Georgina thing). Part of me feels like donning sunglasses and pretending to talk into the hand-held radio. "We've got a 6-9 in progress on Amor Avenue. Over." The grown-up part of me resists, however, given the seriousness of the situation. Jacob and Ben don't look down for jokes right now. They don't have my giddy reaction to stress. When he parks, Ben turns to us.

"No talking. No interfering." His eyes flash to me.

"What?" I cross my arms defensively. I'm not planning to interfere. Unless the police insist on arresting Luke. Which would be a mistake.

"Wait in the lobby while I get this settled. Then, I'll ask to use a conference room and get your statements."

We walk inside and Jacob and I get to sit next to a pimply teenage gnome who's handcuffed to his seat.

"Careful," an officer calls to us across the room. "That one has sticky fingers!"

The gnome sticks his tongue out at the officer and turns his back on us.

I sit and wait. And wait. My feet start tapping the floor of their own accord. So many unanswered questions.

Jacob's phone rings. He answers and walks away. It's clear he's talking to Saffron. I hear the shriek when he tells her we're at the police station. He walks outside, trying to calm her down.

The gnome next to me starts fumbling with something. I realize the bottle cap bracelet Ben gave me is gone.

"You could keep that, but it's got a recording spell on it. I'll hear everything you say," I tell the little twerp.

"You dropped it."

"You're lying."

"You're lying."

"Guess there's one way for you to find out. Can't wait to hear your next convo with your girlfriend. Play it for your parents." I wink.

He drops the bottle cap like it's covered in acid. I lean over and scoop it up. I stare at it a second. Right now, it's only legal to use because I've consented to be Ben's informant. But that assumes people will confess the crime to me. Unlikely. How could I record them without them talking directly to me?

Ben would say we need a search warrant to plant a spelled device. But he's so by-the-book. What if my bracelet just happened to fall off? What if I really did drop it? Into someone's purse? Or into a box? Say a box of things from Georgina's apartment? What if it was an accident?

I stare at the bottle cap. I'm not sure my legal argument would hold up in court. But if I could get us a lead … now a different dilemma plagues me.

Who do I try to record? Luke? Or Saffron?

Neither of them were the man on the fire escape. But both have strong motives for killing Georgina. And Luke was leaving with a box of things from her place tonight. That makes his story about breaking up months ago seem like a bunch of baloney. But Jacob heard Saffron ask to delay a search warrant. That's gotta be worse, right? If the draining thing is true, a vamp's more likely to be involved than a thunderbird. But if Georgina was doing something else …

I chew my lip, debating.

Jacob walks in the front door with Saffron just as Ben walks out from the back of the station with Luke. It's now or never.

Saffron rushes over and gives me a hug. I see Jacob's face behind her. The pain. The distrust. The decision is easy. I slip my bracelet discreetly into her large purse. Even if it's inadmissible, Jacob needs the truth. I can't let him go through life wondering if his wife was involved in a murder. Heck, I need the truth.

"I'm okay." I tell Saffron. "We just saw a fire. We're just witnesses this time. I'll be back."

I head over to Luke and Ben. I ask Ben for his car keys.

"You know my policy on giving you keys."

"I need to give Luke his box of stuff."

"I'll come with you."

I roll my eyes and follow the guys down to the parking garage.

Luke hangs back so I slow my steps to walk beside him.

"Are you okay?" I ask.

"Yeah. Just can't believe it. Did they get Mr. Knight out?"

"I dunno. Not before we left. Three firefighters went in. I saw one come out. But not sure."

Bennett shoves a box into Luke's hands. "Hawkins."

"Do you know if Mr. Knight made it?" Luke turns to Ben.

"Hoping he didn't?"

I smack Ben's arm. I can't help thinking his hostility toward Luke is misplaced. He glares at me. I glare right back.

Ben sighs. "Channel Thirteen's already reporting it. Knight didn't get out. They'll have to send in a phoenix specialist to I.D. the ashes." A phoenix can comb through the ashes to identify other creatures. Something to do with their ability to identify one another and prevent reincarnation mix-ups. (I think I read once about some debacle with mixed up ashes. The two phoenixes involved ended up with mismatched wings when they re-formed.)

Luke's eyes tighten with grief at the thought of losing Mr. Knight. "I'm sorry to hear that." He turns to me. "I was wondering if I could talk to you for a sec?"

"Sure."

Ben's eyes snap to each of us. "Two minutes. Then I need your statement, Lyon." He stomps off.

"Yes, dad." I call after him. I roll my eyes. "Sorry."

"He's not my biggest fan I take it."

I shrug. "He thinks you're dangerous. Plus, maybe I'm giving myself too much credit, but I think there's a bit of sour grapes."

Luke's eyes widen. "Wait. Are you saying?" He swivels to look at Bennett's back as the other man wrenches open the station door. "Is he the ex?"

"Yup."

Luke laughs. "No wonder he hates me."

"Well, not like he's got a lot of reason to. Seeing as we only went on one date and there won't be another."

"What?"

I lean forward. Not because I want to stare deeply into his eyes or anything. Only because I want to make a point. "You lied to me about how long ago the break up was."

"I—I know. I didn't want you to think of yourself as a rebound. Because you're not. You're amazing. That was the best date of my entire life. All one hundred and nine years. Ever."

"Do you even understand? You lied. Relationships are based on truth."

"I came by your place with flowers. I was gonna tell you. I promise I was. And I wanted to talk you out of waiting."

I'm stunned. This is the exact opposite of what Bennett told me. He said Luke looked like he was about to break in. Did

Ben see those flowers? Did he know what Luke was actually up to? "When?"

"Last night. I paced the sidewalk. But then I told myself I was being stupid. That you were right and I should wait. I shouldn't bug you with this whole case going on. I should respect your boundaries."

"So what'd you do?"

Luke gives a little grin. "I told your neighbor ladies downstairs that I'd brought flowers for them. I told them I was buttering them up. Because they should expect to see a lot of me really soon."

"Mrs. Snow?"

He shrugs. "I think that was one of them. They were kind of hard to understand. One of them kept putting a hand over her heart and saying something odd, like, 'Oh my dragons!' I think she might have been on something."

I nod, recalling Bennett's display on the balcony. "That's probably Tabby."

Luke reaches out his hand but stops short of touching me. "I know. I won't touch you. But I wanted to tell you the truth."

I nod. But I don't reach for him. It's hard not to give in. But right now, he's right. I'm in the middle of this investigation. And he's still one of my prime suspects. Until this is over, I'm not gonna be able to tell him the truth about everything either. "I appreciate you telling me the truth."

He sighs. "Did I ruin my chances?"

"The flowers help. God, Mrs. Snow will probably bug me about you every day now."

He grins. "I'll be sure to keep sending her flowers then."

"But you're right. I need to get this murder case off my shoulders before I can think straight."

"So this isn't goodbye?"

"Not completely. Not yet."

His smile is so bright it's almost blinding. I have to tear myself away.

But it's time to go make a statement to my ex. A couple statements. One on and one off the record.

CHAPTER 16

I smack open the door to the parking garage. It's very satisfying to see Ben jump. "Spying?"

"Making sure you were safe. Where's your bottle cap bracelet?"

I shrug. "It fell off."

His eyes narrow. "It fell off?"

"Yup."

"How convenient."

"How convenient was it when you told me Luke was looking to rob my apartment?"

He blushes.

"Yeah. I didn't know it was common practice for burglars to bring flowers to their victims. Is that how you knew?"

"Ly—listen."

"No. You listen. You keep interfering in my life. I don't know why. But it needs to stop—"

"I love you." The words spill out of his mouth. I think it's as much a shock to him as it is to me.

"Excuse me?"

Instead of the panic I expect to see, Bennett is calm. "This is not how I wanted to tell you."

"I would hope not." I'm sarcastic. But inside, I feel vulnerable. Like the hard shell I built around myself after our breakup is starting to crack. "I think that phrase is the last thing in the world I expected to hear from you. Especially since after I said it to you, we broke up."

Bennett runs a hand over his face and glances down the hallway. I'm not sure if he's looking to escape, like he did the time I accidentally let those words slip out, four months into our friendship-turned-relationship.

Too soon? Yeah, I admit it. It was a slip of the tongue, okay? Heat of the moment. But I did not expect to get so painfully blasted for it. That night, he literally flew out my window.

Now his feet don't move. He takes a deep shuddering breath. "I've gone rogue."

I gasp. Okay. So maybe *that's* the last thing I expected to hear. Like ever. Momma's boy is rogue? Rogue dragons break from their families. From the strict hierarchy created by centuries of hiding and escaping knights and saints and kings. Rogues live alone. They have more freedom. But they lose the protection of their clan.

At least, that's what I've heard. Every magical creature clamps down hard on the actual rules and powers of their kind. Kind of unspoken law. Don't tell and make yourself vulnerable.

So, seems like Bennett's finally grown a pair and left the nest.

"That's why you moved. But, why does that excuse you being creepy A.F.?"

"It doesn't."

"Right. It doesn't. And you have no excuse for standing behind doors listening to my private conversations!" I shove at his chest.

"I don't want you near him because he's dangerous!"

"Right now the only person in danger is you. I'm so mad at you—" But my voice cracks. My eyes are filling with tears. Dammit. He's broken through my self-control. How can he stand there so calm and shit! Asswipe. It's not fair. You don't get to say all that stuff and then not even fight!

"Ly ..." his voice is soft, like he's calming a wild animal.

Which he kinda is. My heart is beating out of my chest right now.

He reaches for my hand. But I back away.

"I … need to think about this."

"Yeah. Okay. Yeah."

The hiss of static interrupts us. Bennett's pocket is making noise.

"What's that?" I have never been so glad of a distraction in my entire life.

Bennett pulls out a pair of ear buds. "I thought you said you'd lost the bracelet."

I shrug and grab an ear bud out of his hand. "I did." I stuff the ear bud into my ear without further explanation. Let him think it's a coincidence. Right? Plausible deniability and all that?

Saffron's voice drifts over my ear bud and I watch Ben stuff the mate into his ear. I hear crickets chirping in the background. Saffron must be outside.

"I wanted to let you know there's been a fire at Georgina's apartment." A pause. She must be on the phone. "You didn't have anything to do with it did you? … Swear to me."

Bennett and I stare at one another. Who does Saffron think

might have burned down Georgina's place? Unless she knows who the killer is.

Saffron says the next words in a harsh whisper. "Well, I don't know what to think. Georgina died after your guys touched her—I pushed down that search warrant because you said your collection notices—yeah, well my husband was there at the fire. He saw a guy climbing out the window. You have about a hundred goons—well, maybe it *is* what I think of you. Jacob almost died!" We hear a click. Saffron's done on the phone.

Ben's eyes turn to me. "What a convenient place to lose that bracelet."

I shrug.

He gestures for me to proceed down the hall in front of him. "Sounds like Saffron just fell out with her partner in crime. Hopefully, that means she's ready to talk."

"Hopefully."

I stride up the hallway, glad to have a clear direction—on the murder case at least.

"Our other conversation isn't over Ly-ly," Ben's whisper drifts over my neck.

"I know," I grit my teeth as we emerge onto the main floor of the police station. I just have no clue what to say. Or even think. The personal issue is going to require massive dissection with JR. And a couple bottles of wine.

In front of me, Jacob looks like he could use a drink. His face is patched, and his eyes are haggard. I give him a hug. Saffron walks up just then and it's all I can do to resist giving her a death glare.

Bennett joins the happy group. "I've got a conference room lined up. I'll need to take some statements."

"I'll wait in the lobby, hon," Saffron tells Jacob.

"Actually, Judge Watts, if you don't mind joining us, I'd like to take your statement too."

She raises her eyebrows but doesn't comment as we make our way into the conference room. Ben stops for a sec and has a word with an officer before opening the door and ushering us toward a large table.

Jacob and I tell our versions of the fire episode. While we're talking, a police officer opens the door and sticks his head into the room. He gives Ben a thumbs up before popping back out. No explanation.

Ben ignores my raised brows. Instead, he turns to Saffron.

"Judge Watts, are you aware the station is surrounded by spelled surveillance?"

"I—" she definitely goes pale. "I believe I may have forgotten that."

"I believe you may have," Bennett fights a smirk. I'm about to give a mini fist pump under the table because Ben found a way to collect the evidence of her conversation legally.

But I see Jacob's expression as he watches his wife. My hand stills. Instead I reach for his hand and give it a squeeze.

"Judge Watts, may I ask who you were on the phone with just now?"

Saffron's look is pure panic. "I plead the fifth and demand an attorney immediately."

"Judge Watts, I haven't accused you of anything yet. I was hoping to get a statement from you." Ben pauses a moment to see if Saffron will relent. She doesn't. "Unfortunately, on your phone conversation just now, you admitted to pushing down a search warrant."

"I—I—" she sputters.

"You'll be charged with obstruction of justice at a minimum. I doubt Gruff will want to keep on a judge with ethical issues. I have no doubt the voting public will take great interest in a City Council candidate with an open case—"

Saffron turns pleading eyes to Jacob.

Jacob is stoic. Still. She breaks.

"I've … been having an affair with Matthew Boolye. That's who was on the phone."

CHAPTER 17

Jacob drops my hand. I turn to look at him. He stands
and shifts, shredding the clothes he's wearing. I stand
up and pull open the door for his coyote. I look at Ben.
"I'm going too."

Ben nods and tosses me his keys. I tilt my head in question.
He waves me off as Saffron collapses with a sob.

I turn to follow Jacob, but he's already made it outside. A
lone howl fills the night with heartbreak.

There is no way I can keep up with Jacob in coyote form. I
let him run it out and call a Broomer to bring me back to his
house. I wait on the stoop and stare at the stars until he
arrives an hour later.

He uses a spell associated with his coyote form to let us in the front door.

As he trots off to the bedroom to change I call out after him, "Pack a bag. You're sleeping at my place."

He doesn't respond, but I assume he's following orders. I search his living room where I do indeed find my phone stuck between the couch cushions.

I text Bennett. *Taking Jacob to my place. You can come by to grab your keys whenever.*

He texts back. *Going to see Matthew Boolye. And those are your keys now.*

It's just a text, but it sends shivers up my spine. Do I want the key to Bennett's place? Isn't it too soon? Too scary? We haven't even been on a date!

I desperately want to call JR, but it's mid-evening, they're down a paralegal since I'm out, and if the Saffron obstruction-of-justice gossip has gotten out, they're also down a judge. She's gonna be knee-deep in it.

Another text dings my phone. *Do not freak out Ly. I didn't mean it like that. I meant, those keys are yours because I don't expect to get them back. Loser. Of things.*

Good. Because I already lost the keys, Stalker. I lost them like I lost that bracelet earlier. Hope you enjoy the visit from the big hulking troll I gave them to.

Ha-ha.

Jacob's still not out of the bedroom. I text Ben one more thing. *Did you formally charge Saffron?*

I don't get to decide charges Ly. But yeah based on the video, they did.

She in custody?

Lawyered up.

Okay. Thanks.

I don't know how long Jacob and I have until Saffron gets back. We'd better get a move on.

"Jacob!" I clap my hands. He doesn't respond, so I walk into the bedroom. I find him dressed, and human form, slumped over on the bed. For a second, I feel a sense of out-of-body déjà vu. I have the feeling that I looked the exact same way when I found out my dad had brain cancer. Jacob was the one to find me then.

That's how I decide what we need to do next. When Jacob found me, he forced me out of bed and took me to twelve different automotive shops with him while he searched for a part for his vintage Ford Mustang.

"Chop chop! We've got a murder to solve!" I hurry to the closet and throw some random clothes into a duffel bag. Jacob won't be the most fashionable while he stays with me, but I will keep him busy. Damn busy.

I come back out to find him in the same position. "Oh no you don't. You dragged my sorry pouty butt all over kingdom come once upon time. Now you're getting a taste of your own medicine, Mr. Watts." I grab his hand and tug him to follow me.

"Where we going?"

"To Hearts and Powers," I rattle off the name of the Knight family's B&B. The cops have already been there. It's probably a major waste of time. But, right now, I have a lot of time to waste and a coyote shifter to distract.

We grab a couple Broomers, swing by my place to drop off Jacob's stuff and grab my favorite new spy-cam, and we're at Hearts and Powers before you know it.

I've never been here before. As the witches fly off, I know why. It looks like a valentine's card threw up on a house. Gross. It's all pink trim and crushed red velvet drapes and cupid fountains and heart shaped benches. And flowers. Endless amounts of flowers. Daisies. Rose wreaths on every door. I can taste the flowers on my tongue. Like someone assaulted me with a perfume bottle. There are vamps that like this? Hot Vamp could stand this? That's strike two for him in the bad taste department. (One was dating Georgina for those keeping score.)

I have a very very hard time believing that ice-queen Georgina ran this place. Of course, she may not have decorated it. A gnome gardener wanders past carrying a nude cupid.

"Excuse me," I decide to get started with the interrogation, since Jacob's just standing sullenly. "Did you know Georgina Knight?"

He grunts and flips us off.

"I think we met his son at the station earlier," I snark to Jacob. I grab my phone and snap a pic as the gardener bends over in front of the cupid to set him in place. You have to get just the right angle. Yup. Comic gold. Maybe I'll post that on Instagoul later. Hope it gets back to him. Jerk-face.

Jacob does not admire my perfect snapshot. He sighs and stares off into the distance. I punch him in the shoulder and push him toward the steps. "Come on. Maybe we'll have better luck inside."

Most of the staff are reluctant to talk. Until we hit a jackpot with an upstairs maid who's as human and as giggly as they come. My guess is she's also a blood donor. Hopefully that's what's made her light-headed. Not just empty space between the ears. But she's willing to talk, so we take what we can get. "Oh, yeah. Ms. Georgina was always a grump. You know, I always wondered why she ran this place. Not really her style you know?"

I roll my eyes. "You are not kidding."

"I think her mom designed it all."

"That would make sense. Their house was always so ... baroque." It's all I can do to stop myself from saying gaudy. But yeah. That would technically be the right word. I wasn't over there often, but enough to appreciate that Adelia Knight had way way too much time and money on her hands. Eternal-life problems.

"Yeah, Ms. Knight and her mom didn't really seem to agree on a lot of things. They were always snapping at each other." She puts a hand to her chest. "Which I get, because my mom's getting on my case about moving out. But geez. They were constant. Ms. Georgina was always saying: 'Let me take care of it.' 'I can handle it. Dad put me in charge. And I'm handling it.' That was the latest. Her mom didn't want her taking on some big project or something. Helicopter mom, for sure."

I bite my lip. I don't remember the helicopter part. But then, maybe losing Alec changed Mrs. Knight.

"Would you say Georgina and Adelia hated each other?"

The maid shrugs. "I really dunno. I know they were dramaville. But that's about it."

I thank her and Jacob and I head off downstairs. "What dya' think?"

"Should I have taken Saffron to a place like this?" He stares sadly at a painting of a couple hand-in-hand under a tree.

I put an arm around him. "Jacob, you are an amazing person.

You didn't do anything wrong. When someone has an affair, it's usually about them. Their low self-esteem. Their own issues."

"But she didn't come to me. With her issues."

"No."

"We're supposed to be best friends."

"I know." What else can I say? She should have gone to him. And she's a big fat jerk-face. But getting angry won't help Jacob. I push him toward the exit.

A fairy working the front desk starts to flutter our way, but I wave her off. "We're on our way out. Thanks."

I pull open the front door to come face to face with Adelia Knight.

She looks pale (paler than normal for a vampire, if such a thing is possible). I haven't spoken to her in years. But she just lost the last two members of her family. I should say something, right? "Mrs. Knight, I'm so sorry for your loss."

She glances up at me. "I'm sorry. Do I know you?"

"I used to date Alec. A long long time ago."

She stares at me for a second and tilts her head. "Who— What? I'm sorry." Her eyes look empty. I'm not even sure she heard me.

Jacob's puts a hand on my shoulder and firmly steers me away. "Beautiful place, ma'am. Have a nice night."

Mrs. Knight doesn't respond.

Jacob sighs next to me. "I think I've got it bad. It could always be worse."

True. So true. I've been charged with a murder—but it looks like Matthew Boolye did it and Ben's finally hunting down the right suspect. On the other hand, I have a terrible choice to make. Or a delicious choice. Depending on perspective. Ben or Luke? Still, none of my problems—even when I sat in the dungeon cell—add up to anything close to what Adelia Knight has gone through.

"You know what I think we need?" I say.

"Ice-cream," Jacob answers.

"Hey! You weren't supposed to guess."

"You always want ice-cream. Or jellybeans. Or some kind of cavity-inducing, mouth-rotting—"

"Okay, okay. We can order you something from Nom-Noms." It's a little golem restaurant I love because they're open and have dessert twenty-four/seven. Because golems never sleep.

"They have meat?"

"Yes. They even have rabbit." I roll my eyes.

Jacob and I have just settled down on my purple couch with delicious takeout boxes when Bennett calls.

"Matthew didn't do it unless he hired it out." He doesn't even greet me.

"Well, hello to you, too."

"The camera he blocked off at Abra the night of Georgina's death showed he and Saffron making out." I stand up and move quickly away from Jacob. I go out onto my balcony.

"You watched it?" I suppress a shiver. Matthew has always grossed me out. I can't believe Saffron would touch him.

"Twice."

"Puke?"

"Considered it. But thought it would be unprofessional."

"What about the fire?"

"He has an alibi. An actual meeting with his accountant. His assistant was there too."

"Could he have hired someone?"

"Not according to his accountant. He's broke. Between construction and the campaign, he stretched himself too thin. It's why he was writing threatening notes to Georgina. Trying to get her to cough up a loan repayment early."

"That's why Saffron blocked the search warrant?"

"Yup. He thought it would look bad."

"He's right."

"Yeah. But doesn't make him a murderer."

"Adultery is just as bad."

"Unfortunately, not illegal. Even if it was, I'm still left with a murder case to solve."

Damn. "Well then what? Dad did it, felt bad and offed himself?"

He sighs into the phone. "Maybe. I gotta get back to the office to see the phoenix report and your infrared photos. There's still always jealous ex-boyfriend with Crypt connections."

"I don't like that theory much."

"I know."

We stay in silence on the line for a bit. And strangely, it's a comfortable silence.

"Think we'll figure it out before my next arraignment?"

"I hope so."

"Me too. Listen, Jacob's here and then later I have dinner with JR ..."

"Okay. I'll let you go. But Ly ..."

"Yeah?"

"Our prior conversation's still not over." This time his voice is breathy.

"Okay," I squeak and hang up. I can't tell if I'm nervous or giddy. Maybe both.

Even after we eat, Jacob is in no fit state to be left alone. I have to figure out a way to perk him up before I go to torture-over-lobster later—the only meat good on its own because it's naturally sweet—and yes, I'm making JR shell out the big bucks for putting me through said torture. I do debate taking Jacob with me, but he really doesn't need to be subjected to Liam's negativity right now.

Instead, I tell him to hold his nose and we head downstairs.

I don't even finish knocking on Mrs. Snow's door before she opens. Surprisingly, Tabby's there again. The smell that wafts out is more like peanut butter cookies than rat innards. I sigh in relief.

"Oh my, sugar, your young man is just the sweetest thing."

"No," Tabby interjects, pulling a kindergarten-teacher sweater over her shoulders. She sticks her hands into the apple-shaped pockets as she retorts, "I dunno who the dragon-shifter was, but girl, if you don't want him, he's mine."

Mrs. Snow claps. "We've been here since it all happened. My bunco group came over and we all had a nice chat about which one you'd choose."

I nod slowly. My personal life has just become prime gossip for a group of retired women with nothing better to do. And one of them owns a crystal ball and has been known to peep.

Note to self. Move. Break all crystal balls in town. Or never have sex again. If that's even an option. I haven't even kissed either one. But now I'm paranoid. I don't want them watching me. Unless … if Tabby only likes shifters, maybe I choose Luke. But my conversation with Bennett makes Luke the prime suspect again.

I realize the women have stopped talking and everyone's staring at me, waiting for introductions.

"Mrs. Snow, Ms. Blue, this is Jacob Watts," I say.

Jacob politely shakes hands with both women and I think I see Tabby blush.

"Did you wanna see the flowers Luke left, yeah?" Mrs. Snow asks as she ushers us inside.

"Oh. Um, sure."

Her dining table has a bouquet of white lilies and roses on it. Normally, I'd say it's gorgeous. But after Hearts and Powers, I'm a little flowered out. "It's nice," I shrug nonchalantly.

"Nice! Girl, you have a thing or two to learn." Mrs. Snow

lectures as she goes to grab a pitcher of lemonade and a platter of peanut butter cookies.

We sit at the dining table, but the flowers block me from making eye contact. I move them to the floor.

"I actually came to see if you ladies still have that crystal ball," I try to keep my voice calm and even. "Jacob and I are looking into a murder." I phrase it carefully. I do not say investigating. I don't officially have any authority to investigate. And I definitely do not say that we're investigating a murder I've been charged with. God, that would get the lips flapping. The bunco ladies would probably permanently move in and take turns patrolling me.

Tabby's jaw drops.

Mrs. Snow misses her mouth and spills lemonade on the table.

"A murder!"

"You don't mean that young man we saw last time, do you?" Tabby asks, worried about Bennett.

"No. No. He's fine," I hope. "I'm not really sure how to say this, but someone thinks Luke might be involved in a murder." I gesture to the flowers to remind them of my other gentleman-caller.

Like a comedy movie, both women's hands fly to their hearts. "No!"

I nod sadly. "I think that person is a little *crazy*. But I just met Luke and you never know—"

Tabby nods. "It's true. Men can lie. I once dated a shifter who said he was a bob-cat. Three months later I found out he was a nasty little no-haired sphynx cat."

Mrs. Snow curls her lip. "Awful."

Jacob, shockingly, joins in. "Yeah, people can lie to your face. And you sometimes don't even know."

Both women look at Jacob and turn to me. I give a tiny nod. They nod in return—acknowledging we have an active heartbreak on our hands. Tabby pats Jacob's hand sympathetically.

Mrs. Snow pounds the table. "Well, that's it then. Let's grab that ball and take a look at Luke. We gotta prove that boy's innocence so he can come courtin'."

Tabby's back with a crystal ball in no time. She plops it onto the middle of the table, setting up some tropical-themed coasters as blocks to keep it from rolling around. She cracks her knuckles. "So, we're just looking for Luke? Easy enough." She closes her eyes.

Two seconds later, the ball is glowing.

Luke and Cherry Jones pop into view. They're sitting in a cramped office with a bald witch doctor, who's waving a skull around in one hand and throwing some nasty-looking orange water on Luke's face.

"Nope. Not sheeing anything." The witch doctor has a nasty lisp that verges on a whistle. And he slurps his own spittle before he speaks again. "No love shpells. You're free and clear."

Luke leans back in his chair with a sigh. Cherry offers him a towel and he wipes the orange liquid off his face. He tosses a bag of gold onto the table. The witch doctor grabs it, packs his bag, and bows himself out.

"So, it's real." Luke sits back in this chair. "I actually like this girl."

Cherry leans forward. "After what G did to you. To us. I think we both deserve some happiness. I'm happy for you, Luke."

He grins at her across the desk. But Cherry's violet eyes start to grow big and pleading.

"But—" he says slowly.

"But, that ceremony just means you like her. It doesn't mean she likes you. For all we know she could be using you."

Luke rolls his eyes. "What could Lyon possibly want?"

"She's been accused of G's murder." Mrs. Snow and Tabby both gasp and look up at me. I hold my hands up in the universal protest of innocence. I want to glare at Cherry for outing me. But that wouldn't do any good.

"She didn't do it," Jacob whispers to the women. For some reason, the word of a stranger calms them down.

"There is no way that girl is a murderer," Luke's voice is loud and clear.

I feel myself swell up with pride at the way he defends me. But then I check myself. What the heck am I doing feeling pride that someone doesn't think I'm a murderer? I'm not. Hello. That's not something to be proud of. That's a given. I mentally smack myself before staring back at the ball.

"Even if she's not, she'll be desperate to find out who is. And if she gets wind of the kid—"

Kid—what kid? The wicked witch had a kid?

"Adelia would never let that get out. It would ruin the family. Besides she loves that kid too much."

"So you say. But now G's dad's gone too. How do ya think that happened?"

"Don't be so paranoid."

"Don't get so wrapped up in this girl so quick."

"I'm not."

Her eyes grow even bigger. "I just don't want to see you get hurt."

Luke snorts. "Knock it off, Cher. That doesn't work on me."

"Too bad," she flutters her eyelashes.

The light in the ball fades as Luke pulls open the door to the office and leaves.

Mrs. Snow turns to me. "Investigating a murder, huh?"

"Trying to clear my name."

Both women open their mouths at the same time. I hold up a hand. "Jacob can explain. It might take him awhile. I have to go make a phone call. And then go to dinner. Do you mind if he stays here?"

Tabby looks excited. Mrs. Snow—ever the southern lady—can't refuse an opportunity to play hostess.

They flutter around him, asking questions.

He gives me a death glare and mouths, "You owe me," over their heads.

I wiggle my fingers at him. He might hate me but keeping busy-bodies at bay is better than moping. I've left him in capable, if overeager, hands.

I pull out my phone, scroll through my contacts, until I reach 'Monkey Butt Licker' aka Bennett French. Might be time to rename that contact. I hit dial. It rings. He doesn't answer. Screw it.

He won't answer? I'll go find him.

CHAPTER 18

I walk past Arnold the asshat supervisor on my way to Bennett's office.

"You aren't supposed to be here."

"I'm not here for work."

He stares me down as though I owe him an explanation as to why I'm near the courthouse at all. I bite down on my tongue in order to keep it in my mouth. Sometimes, I think I deserve a medal for dealing with such a butt-munch on a daily basis. Why are bosses always such jerk-offs? Is that part of the test to get promoted to supervisor? Seriously.

When Arnold doesn't get his explanation, he huffs and continues on down the hall. I roll my eyes.

I knock before entering Bennett's office. He's hunched over a series of photos, a huge book of runes opened beside him. He has a soggy meatball sandwich in one hand and a photo in the other.

"How's it going?"

He looks up, startled. A meatball plops out of his sandwich onto the pictures.

"Crap! Ly, I didn't hear you."

"I knocked."

"I was just—" he blots at the mess and scarfs down the meatball that fell (gross) and gestures at his pile. "I've been trying to figure out what these damn runes mean."

I take a seat and pull a couple of photos toward me. Among the blackened mess that was Georgina's apartment, there are at least five runes glowing like embers. "How long have you been doing this?"

"Like two hours."

"Don't you have a witch on staff?"

"Yeah."

"Call her in here."

"She's not on the case."

"You don't need her on the case."

Ben gives me the evil eye. But I wave him off.

"Trust me. Who told you about infrared pictures? Who's gotten you every lead on this case so far? In fact, I think you should pay me. I'm pretty much doing your job for you—"

Bennett grumbles and reaches for his phone. "I still don't know how you knew about that infrared thing."

"I had an interesting cellmate when I was improperly arrested and imprisoned while unconscious," I retort.

He asks the witch, Amy, to come over to his office.

"Now, why did I do that?" he asks as he puts down his phone.

"If you were a girl, you'd never have asked that question."

When Amy enters, I hand her a photo. "Did you ever do the match spell in high school?"

She grins. "Like every other day."

"Bennett doesn't know what the match spell is."

Amy turns to him. "It's only like the best spell to find the dress to go with your perfect shoes. Or vice versa."

"Shoes?" Mr. French looks like he doubts my brilliant plan.

"The spell finds things that go together," I explain to him before turning to Amy. "Can you match the pictures of these runes with the definitions in the book?"

"Easy peasy."

She closes her eyes, whispers the spell, snaps, and flip! Voila!

Bennett's book is open on the page with the correct rune. I grab the photo from her and stick it into the book to mark the page.

"Amazing." I enjoy watching Bennett's shocked face. I could get used to that. I make a mental note to try to get him to make that face as often as possible.

"Amy, we have a few more." I hand her another.

Amy matches the remaining four runes and leaves after Bennett and I have thanked her. I promise her Ben owes her donuts tomorrow and she seems pretty happy. Ben doesn't seem quite so amused by my generosity on his behalf.

"I don't want my people thinking rewards are a thing," he scolds me.

"But they are a thing," I quip.

"Not from me."

"Okay, *Arnold*." I roll my eyes. See, supervisors equal jerks. Am I right?

Bennett ignores me and flips open the rune dictionary. "To stay… to hide … to subdue… to conceal … to forget."

My eyes widen. "Those sound serious. Like Georgina was doing something illegal. And hiding it. The reporter said neighbors heard strange noises from that apartment."

Ben's eyes flicker up to mine. And I can tell, immediately, that he's hiding something.

"What is it?"

He bites his lip. Lust flares up, but I push it down. The case is too serious right now for that. We're on the cusp of something. I can feel it.

"What is it?" I repeat.

"I think she was doing something illegal."

"Do you think ... draining?" My voice is weak. I remember why I came here. Luke and Cherry mentioned a kid. "Oh holy night." Do not let G have been draining kids. Do not let that be true.

Ben sighs. "I don't think so. Draining's quick. The biggest problem with a drain is body disposal. These runes, and the chains in her walls make me think it's something even worse."

"Chains?" The blood drains from my face.

"She had chains in one of the bedrooms. Thick chains that spanned the length of the room. Gave access to a bathroom. But not the window. I think Georgina was holding someone prisoner."

A shiver crawls like a spider down my spine. That's so effin' creepy. Like monster-vampire-nightmare creepy. "Who?"

"Well, her father's ashes were found mixed into those chains."

"She chained up her father?"

"No. She couldn't have. I interviewed the parents, remember? They were no help."

"So, she'd chained up someone else?"

"I think so. But clearly, they escaped."

"I heard rumors she had a kid." I'm not sure of the legality of spying on Luke. So I'm vague.

"Vamps can't have kids."

"She turned a kid, maybe? I dunno. It was just a rumor."

"I haven't heard anything like that. Who'd you hear it from?"

I wince. "Luke."

Ben growls. "When did you see him?"

I bite my lip and admit to spying. Ben is much more forgiving of my illegal peeping than he should be. Is that relief on his face? I'm not sure. But whatever it is, I'm glad I'm not getting my ass chewed.

"Why would she turn a kid? Vamps hate kids. They're too human. And dirty. And all that. Luke has to be wrong."

"I think you just want him to be wrong."

"I think you just want to have blinders on when it comes to him."

"This is about a kid. Not him."

"Well, here's the thing. Why would Georgina run for office if she had a vamp kid? They're eternally little terrors. She wouldn't have time to campaign. She would have to take care of it—"

"She did cancel all the dinners at her house. Cherry told me that." I offer.

He shakes his head. "I just don't see it."

"Yeah, well she ran Hearts and Powers and that didn't seem to fit her ice-queen personality much either."

Ben rolls his eyes. "I'll look into it."

"Good."

"So what's your working theory about all this? One murderer? Two separate murders?"

Bennett shrugs. "Now, that's the big question isn't it? Are the two related? Did someone kill Georgina? Did that person go into her apartment intending to kill Mr. Knight? Or did they go in to set the fire and then just have to kill him because he was a witness?"

"Who would do that?"

He laughs. "Well, when you figure it out, you've solved the case."

"You don't have any leads?"

He shakes his head. "Whoever did it was smart. The construction rubble and the fire make evidence collection a bitch."

"And you're for sure it's not Matthew?" I know it's wrong but part of me hates him so much right now, that I wouldn't mind seeing him go down for this.

Bennett comes around his desk to perch on the edge, close enough that our knees almost touch. I can feel his body heat and I have to suppress a tremor of lust. "Unless his accountant is lying. But, he doesn't have much reason to lie. How's Jacob?"

I shrug. "I left him in the gossipy hands of my elderly downstairs neighbor and her friend, who are probably dissecting my love-life right now because Luke gave them flowers and they saw you shift—they were mildly impressed, by the way—so I'm hoping he's reasonably distracted and focused on his annoyance at me right now. Instead of other things."

"Hold on. Back up. Mildly impressed?" Ben slides down so our knees are touching.

My breath catches. Our eyes meet. My mouth rambles. "One of them might have mentioned she'd be interested. I could give her your number if you want? She's seventy. Think she's part cat-shifter."

He gives a half-grin. "Unfortunately, I'm only interested in one woman."

My heart stops as he leans forward. "Should we continue our conversation now, Lyon?"

His green eyes are inches from mine. And they're burning with desire. I see the dragon's flame leap in his irises. Heat and magic engulf me, pulse around me. I lean forward, entranced.

"You know, if you use magic, it's cheating."

"I don't mind cheating to win you over. But I promise you I would never ever do what Saffron did. I won't cheat any other way."

"And… you killed it." I scoot back in my seat.

"What? I'm telling you I'll be loyal."

"Yeah, in the worst way possible."

"I'm sorry."

I sigh. "Me too."

"Can I tell you that you look beautiful?"

I laugh. "The mood's gone. Dead. Vanished. Vamoosed. Exiled—"

Ben cuts me off as he hauls me to my feet. He whirls me around and pushes me up against his desk, wedging his body between my legs. His hands travel up my back, my neck. He traces the edge of my jaw. He nuzzles my ear. And suddenly I can't think. My blood is pounding. And his lips are close. So close.

"Do you know why I went rogue?"

"Why?"

"Because of you." Ben stares at me with such intensity, I can't keep eye contact.

"What are you talking about?"

"They wanted to arrange a match. For me. But when you said you loved me … it changed things. Me."

Tears fill my eyes. He cannot be serious. When I said that, we broke up. "Ben, if this is an effin' joke, it's not funny."

He grabs both my hands, linking our fingers. I should pull it away, but I don't. I'm too busy trying to hold it together inside. Deep breath. Deep breath.

"Look, when you said that, I freaked out. I flew off. But not home. I flew to Japan."

"And what? Had your eastern spiritual awakening? Come on, Ben—" I move to push him away, but he just presses his body into mine.

"No. I realized that I wanted to have some say in my life. When you said those words ... it made me think about the future. About the possibility."

"You flew away."

"I know."

"No. You flew away. Then you showed up wanting to talk for ten years and psychoanalyze why I might have said those words to you."

"When you slammed a door in my face, I might add."

"Darn straight I did. And then you sent me that note."

"I know."

"You said you never wanted to see me again."

"I needed the clan to take my claim seriously. My mom wasn't going to accept my challenge to go rogue at first."

"What are you talking about?"

"She didn't take us seriously. Said you were too young and I was too stupid. After you said *that*, it made me realize that I wanted choices. I wanted to have the ability to choose you if that's what I wanted. But my mom thought I was being irrational. She wasn't going to let me into the arena to fight to go rogue."

"What arena? What fight?"

Ben sighs. "They don't just let you out, Ly. I had to fight every male in the clan."

"What?"

"It took me almost two years. To fight and beat each of them."

My mind is going blank. I see Ben in front of me. But at the same time, I don't. What? I mean WHAT? There are like thirty, maybe thirty-five males in his clan. "But that would mean you just finished."

"Yeah," his voice is quiet. "Three weeks ago."

I stare at him, at a loss for words.

The kiss he gives me shatters any thoughts I might have had. Any witty comebacks are swallowed as lips press mine. Again. And again.

When he releases me, I'm gasping.

He steps back with an arrogant little grin. "The mood was gone, huh?"

I touch my lips, the sensation of his kiss still lingers. "Huh?"

"French, for the win."

I shove him. "Get over yourself."

"That was hot, and you know it."

I roll my eyes and pull his keys out of my purse. "Here. For the record, I didn't lose them."

"For the record, I said you can keep them."

"I don't feel comfortable—"

"Ly, you let lots of neighbors have your keys, right?"

"Only because I need them too."

"Well, I'm rogue. Maybe I need someone to have my extra key." He holds eye contact, not backing down.

"As long as that's all this is," I glance at the key and back up at him.

"That's all this is ... for now," he mutters the last part under his breath.

"I heard that!"

"What?" He ushers me out the door. "Now, get outta here, woman. I have a case to solve."

"You'd better."

"What?"

"Solve this case. I do not wanna go back to the dungeon."

His hand is on my cheek. "I promise, Ly. You won't." Then, Mr. Shovey-hands pushes me out the door.

CHAPTER 19

I t's three a.m. I gave JR as long as I reasonably could, given that I wanted to call her at like ten.

But my insides are about to bust into outsides with the way my anxiety is pushing on them. Of course, the single vamp I've looked at in almost a decade had to check to see if I put a love spell on him. Then he knew about some secret kid Georgina had. . . And to top it all off, I just had the world's hottest makeout session with a dragon whose photo used to serve as my drunken dart-board. My libido is cheering. But my head is spinning. I need someone to talk sense into me.

I sneak down to the District Attorney's floor which is two flights below Ben's office. I creep down the hall to check the paralegal's room. Arnold's in his office. The door's shut, but I'd recognize his yell anywhere.

I keep my body hidden, but peek around the corner. "JR!" I whisper-yell.

She doesn't look up.

I creep over to the recycling bin. It's locked, because you know, everyone is so fascinated by legal documents that they want to come up to our office to steal them. I stick my hand into the slot we use to feed the paper in. Normally the thing is filled to overflowing. Of course, I have to pick the one day it's not. I lean over farther. I just need enough to make some spitballs. My foot slips.

My arm slides farther into the hole and I feel the pinch of plastic. "H-E-double hockey sticks!" My arm is stuck. Of course it is. Because that's my shit luck in life. Damn it all.

I reach for my phone.

I dial JR. The call goes to voicemail. I dial again. And again. And again.

"This better be you frickin' calling from the hospital," she whispers into the phone. "Alfred's having apoplectic fits about all the cases we're going to have to reschedule and all the defense motions to dismiss we have to respond to. There have literally been like eighteen of those just tonight— because of this whole Saffron thing. It's made the entire office crazy."

"Ben said he loved me and Luke had a witch doctor check to see if I put a love spell on him and my arm is stuck in the recycle bin around the corner," I rush to get it all out before she hangs up on me.

Silence.

"Hello?" I check my phone to be sure she hasn't hung up.

"I'm looking at the list of excuses I've used the last couple months on my phone. Do you think he'd buy that my mom was in a Broomer accident?"

I fight tears and a smile. "Might be a bit of a stretch. Danny drunk?"

"Used that one last month when we went shoe shopping."

"Vet called and said your dog ate someone else's dog."

"That doesn't even make sense."

"It would if your dog was a zombie."

She laughs. "I can always go with the stereotypical female standby."

Together we chorus, "Lady problems."

"I'll figure it out. Try to get your arm out. I'll meet you in the restroom." JR commands.

I pull on the recycling bin. "It's pretty stuck."

She sighs. "Turn it on its side. Then you don't have to fight gravity."

I slowly lower what feels like a million pounds of paper to the ground, praying that no one walks up behind me. I can't even imagine what they'd think.

JR is a genius. I'm able to slip my arm out. I leave the overturned recycling bin and run for the restroom. I skid to a stop inside.

JR is there two seconds later. I open my mouth but she holds up a hand. "I called my brother and told him we're meeting him at Wanda's Brews."

I pout. "I thought we were getting lobster."

"I thought I'd get to finish my work instead of lying to my boss."

"Fine." I still cross my arms and stomp my foot two-year-old style.

JR laughs and leads me out the door.

We grab a booth at Wanda's and soon have our Salty Bird cocktails in hand.

"Ok, spill those guts, woman," JR commands as she takes a drink.

I do.

Her jaw almost comes unhinged. I think it might hit the table.

"Why the heck do you get two epic selfless guys tripping

over themselves to get next to you? This is so unfair. You should have to share."

I cock my head and look at her. "Perhaps you didn't hear the part where Luke thought I might have put a spell on him or where Ben told me to get lost and I believed it for two years."

"Yeah, he was totally dead to you. That's a hard reality to change."

"No kidding. And the supposed gang thing, not really sure if Ben's making that up. But what if Luke is in the Crypts? Lots of vamps are." I remind her.

"Okay, I guess I'm not one hundred percent jealous."

"You can't be. How can you possibly be when you have the world's sweetest satyr? With that Spanish accent and that black curly hair…"

"Okay. I'm not really jealous." JR smiles at the thought of Danny.

"Good. Because we have more pressing needs than jealousy. Tell me what to do."

"Whoa. I am not drunk enough for that kind of responsibility," she shakes her head.

"But … how do I know who to pick?"

"You've been on one date. Had one kiss! Slow your roll. Priorities, lady. We need to solve this case first."

"True. So true."

We toss ideas back and forth for awhile. But don't have any major revelations before Liam shows up.

He pulls open the door with drama. Wham. Hair toss. Enter. But that's Liam. He's always wanted everybody looking at him. Youngest child syndrome maybe? Or just a drama queen. Who knows.

Liam orders a drink at the bar and then struts to our table. His crisp three-piece suit and sunglasses that cost more than a month's groceries scream 'I'm important!' I stick my finger down my throat in the universal gagging gesture. JR swipes my arm and forces it down as Liam sits.

"I have the most unbelievable news!" Liam begins.

I put a hand on my chest. "You've been accused of murder, too?"

Liam rolls his eyes. "Lyon, don't be ridiculous."

"Oh, but I'm not. I really have been. Arraignment in a week and a half. Spent a night in the dungeon and everything."

Liam looks at JR. "She's trying to rain on my parade isn't she?"

JR nervously sips her drink. "Maybe. But she's telling the truth."

Liam raises an eyebrow at me. "I knew I didn't like you for a reason. Just shows I've got good judgment."

"Careful what you say, I'm a hardened criminal now."

We have a stare down. I think it's kind of fun, but JR looks so nervous that I stop out of pity for her.

"Fine. What's your news?" I sigh dramatically, as if listening to Liam is the most boring thing in the world. Which possibly, it is. Because I don't want to.

"I've been promoted to ... Vice President of Marketing," Liam announces proudly.

"That's great!" JR gushes. "I'm so proud of you."

"Wait," I hold up a hand. "I'm confused. Weren't you a vice president already?"

"Of Operations, not Marketing," he rolls his eyes as if I should understand why this is such a big deal. But I don't.

"Well, then how is it a promotion? It's more like they got sick of you in Ops and shoved you into a different department."

I can see him grit his teeth. I feel a little thrill run through me. I think I'm like five inside right now. I totally am just riling him up. But it's so damn fun.

JR disagrees. "Obviously, Marketing makes more sales, so now Liam's responsible for the growth of the company, right?" She always has to appease him. Big sister soothing baby brother.

I focus back on my drink while Liam preens and tells JR all about his new job. We order and I do my best to keep my tongue from wagging. Partially because JR has her heel grinding into my foot.

"If you'd just move away from here, Juniper, you'd be able to do so much more for yourself." Liam cuts into his steak and his sister at the same moment.

"Can't go one evening without picking on her?" I ask.

"I just want what's best for her."

"You just want her to leave Tres Lunas like you. So she'll be stuck in the human world? Pretending to be something she's not? That's what's best for her?"

"You maggies are all the same," Liam uses a derogatory word for magic-bearers. "The human world isn't bad. It isn't a sham. It's part of what we are."

"She couldn't grow her plants out there."

"She doesn't need to grow plants."

"You don't know what she needs."

"Magic isn't a need, Lyon."

"I know that."

"I don't think you do. Everyone in this little town is stuck in their little bubble. So dependent on magic—wouldn't know how to solve a problem without it if their lives depended on it."

"E.S.A.D." I retort, downing the rest of my drink and waving over the waiter to get me another.

"What was that? Did you just curse me? See … case and point," Liam purses his lips.

JR chuckles. And then busts out laughing. "She just cursed you. But not like that. It's an acronym for eat shit and die."

I don't hold back my laughter. Liam turns very very red. JR and I fall into one of those laugh cycles—where eye contact with the other person just sets you off again. My ribs hurt by the time we're laughed out.

"OMG. That was hilarious," I wipe my eyes on my napkin.

"Glad you find me funny," Liam chips at me.

"Oh, I do. Ranting on about magic. Because every time you get a date it's pure freakin' magic."

"That's it. I've had enough of your anti-human superiority."

He tosses a bill on the table and glares at JR. "Next time don't bring her."

JR waves goodbye feebly. "Congrats again."

Even pissed, Liam manages to strut out and make eyes at the waiter on his way. God, he's such a diva!

I turn back to JR. "Sorry if I ended the evening too soon."

She tosses back her drink and sighs. "Why is family the hardest to get along with?"

"Dunno."

She pulls her hair out of bun she had it in, and sits back, combing through it. "I mean, he's done well for himself. Considering he has like almost no magic. I always felt bad for the kid—"

"Wait," I hold up a hand to her. "What did you say?"

"I said I felt bad for the kid—"

But I cut her off, already standing up.

"WTF. I just figured it out. I gotta go!" I grab my phone and sprint out of the restaurant. I call Ben. He doesn't answer. "Ben—call me back asap! I know who killed Georgina!"

CHAPTER 20

A Broomer drops me off at home. I check downstairs, but no lights are on at Mrs. Snow's. Hopefully Jacob escaped back up to my apartment.

I'm buzzing with nervous energy. I stare at my phone, willing Bennett to call me back.

I climb the stairs. I search my purse for my keys but don't feel them. "Oh no! Not now! I know I had my keys on me—" I check my pockets. There! Thank goodness. I do not want to have to wake anyone up so close to dawn.

I unlock my door and step inside. The balcony doors are open. Maybe Jacob's outside?

I shiver. I need to close the door, but there's no moon

tonight. It's pitch black in here. And freezing. How long has Jacob been out there? I hope he's not sulking—

I shuffle forward toward a lamp. Dammit! I slip. I think on a house key I lost two days ago. I right myself, pull the chain on my reading lamp, and it flickers to life.

I gasp.

Alec Knight sits on my couch with a vicious dagger in his hand. Twenty-five-years-old, blonde curls and plush lips, just like I remember. But he's human, not vamp anymore. Older. Angrier. Much much scarier.

My heart hammers in my chest. It's my worst nightmare come to life.

I can't handle the fearful silence. So like an idiot, I try to break the ice. "Is that a dagger in your hand, or are you happy to see me?"

He doesn't laugh.

A nervous titter slips out of my lips. "Is this a joke?" I can tell by the grim determination in his eyes that it's not.

He slowly stands. "The only one making bad jokes is you."

I get defensive. And that's good—that's better than vulnerable. "Well what do you want me to do? Welcome you into my home? Sit down right here so you can slit my throat a little easier?"

"That would be nice, yes."

"Which one?"

"You know which one." He stands.

"They said you were in Europe." I try to make conversation, while edging behind the love seat. Is Jacob here? Jacob can't be here. I hope he didn't come up here. I keep my eyes on the knife as I try to put distance between Alec and myself.

"Nope."

"Never?"

"My sister liked her little stories. Liked to flesh out my absence. Did you know she even wrote herself postcards and told people they were from me? Her little human brother, who traveled the world."

"She did what?" I act outraged on his behalf, hoping that somehow that will make me seem less murderable. If that's a thing. Damn! What I wouldn't give for ESP or telekinesis or something! Why didn't I tell Ben everything in that damn voicemail! Why did I have to wait and try to be all dramatic and shit! Idiot!

Alec smiles, like he knows what I'm thinking. Like he enjoys watching the panic take over my limbs. He takes another slow step closer.

"I came by your house every day for two years after I

accidentally—you know—changed you." The confession isn't intentional. I don't know why I say it. It just comes out.

He tilts his head. "I know."

"You know? Wait. You were there?"

"Mm-hmm. Having a vamp turn human is shameful, you know. Losing power. Made the family look vulnerable. They never reported me. They locked me up. Wouldn't let me leave the house. Not for nine years. Can you imagine nine years locked up, Ly?"

"The runes were for you." Tears start to fill my eyes and I swipe them away. What are you doing, stupid? Keep your eyes on that knife! Pity and fear fight for control of my body.

"Yeah, until big sister decided to keep me at her place. Then decided keeping me was too much trouble. She was gonna use some unicorn horn to wipe my memory and send me on my way. Elected officials don't have time for shameful family secrets."

"How'd you escape?"

He laughs. "Mommy dearest didn't want her baby boy to forget her. She let me out that night. Expecting me to run."

"So, it was chance that you happened to find me and Georgina at the same place?"

"I like to think of it as divine retribution. You took my powers. You helped me take hers."

"So, we're even."

Alec gives a slow scary smile. "Oh no. We're not. I might have let you go. I knew you were sorry about everything that happened. But you had to keep pushing. Asking my mother questions when I'd just used that powdered unicorn horn on her. Do you know how inconvenient that is?"

"I—what about your dad?" I try to turn the subject away from me. Accusing me of things is a bad, bad topic. It makes him way more likely to jump the couch and kill me. How do the movies do it? Keep the bad guy monologuing? Look intrigued. Ask questions. "Why'd you kill your dad?"

"He knew it was me. Came after me. Found me. Like a human ever has a shot against a vamp."

"Well, you do. Apparently."

A small smirk crosses his face.

"Apparently. He was too arrogant. That was his mistake. He took me to Georgina's place. But he didn't check the runes. My powerful, idiot sister, forgot the rune for silence."

"The neighbors heard you."

He nods.

"Did they have keys?"

"One did. A little old lady shifter."

"She unlocked you."

"Couldn't believe that Georgina was into 'draining humans.'"

"Then what?"

"Then it was just a waiting game until he came back. I got him close, cuffed him. And that was that."

"It was you on the fire escape. You were fast."

Before I can blink, Alec demonstrates his speed. He leaps over the loveseat.

I've never felt full-body paralysis before. But watching Alec jump toward me, death in his eyes, my body just freezes.

This is it. The end—my end. My mind doesn't go into instant replay. Instead, everything I've never done flashes before my eyes. I'll never get married. Never have kids. Grandkids. I'll never make it to Moontop Mountain. Never kiss Bennett again. Never get another date with Luke.

The knife touches my neck. It snaps me out of my daze. I try to focus. I see the key I tripped on—it shimmers in the lamplight. And gives me a startling revelation.

Alec caresses my neck with the knife.

"I'll make yours fast. You didn't mean it. Not like her."

I turn slightly so I can look Alec in the eyes. "I'm sorry for what happened. But I can't let you kill me."

"You don't get much choice." He digs the point of the knife into my neck, just to the side of the artery.

I take a deep breath, hoping against hope that I'm right. "Alec. Get lost."

He disappears. Just like my keys.

The knife clatters to the floor.

I bend over, letting out a rush of air. My right leg burns for some reason. Stress reaction? The emotions are too much. Tears start. I'm brushing them away and hugging myself and shaking like a leaf. I sink to the floor and see a feather. Did Alex stab my pillow?

I rub my leg and eye the knife, my thoughts a jumbled mess.

Bam-bam-bam. Someone pounds on my door. I stagger to my feet and check the peephole.

Alec is in the hall. His fists pummel my door. "What did you do to me? Open up."

I check the lock, make sure the deadbolt is on. Then I slide the chain on too.

I grab my phone and it rings in my hand. Bennett. My fingers are shaking so much I have trouble swiping to answer.

"Hey," his voice is soothing.

"Alec Knight. He did it. He's at my apartment." I choke out the words.

I hear his roar and hold the phone away. I hear an electronic sizzle and wonder if maybe, possibly, he shifted into his dragon and torched his phone. If that means he's on his way, good. I owe him a phone. Two phones. And a couple of dates.

I sink down on my side of the door, ignoring Alec's pounding until it starts to give me a headache.

"I called in the dragons. You might wanna head out."

The pounding on the door stops. Thank effing goodness. I rub my temples.

CHAPTER 21

Bennett and an entire squad of flying shifters arrive to arrest Alec.

He finds me on the floor of my apartment, still shaking. He scoops me up into his arms and carries me to the couch while the police take care of the official business. Eventually, one of the boys in blue wanders my way and wants a statement. I open my mouth to start the long, awful story of my confrontation with Alec, but Ben puts a finger to my lips and plucks at my hair. He holds my spy-cam in front of me.

"Was this on?"

I sag against him in relief and nod. Thank goodness. Because my brain is more fried than an Oreo at the fair.

Bennett hands the tiny clip-on camera to the detective and

says, "Have IT download the video. It'll show you her whole day."

I realize that it means the police will see my illegal crystal ball gazing, my fight with a recycling bin, my moaning over Ben and Luke. I swipe at the camera and wrest it out of the detective's hands. "You know. I think I might want to talk after all."

He sits, and I spill my guts.

YOU KNOW THE ANNOYING THING ABOUT BEING A VICTIM OF A crime like attempted murder?

You have to tell your story again and again.

I talked to the detective. I gave an edited version of the video to the police. But then I had to come back to the courthouse and tell my story again for Bella and the other prosecutors working the case. Gah!

To top it all off, Bennett asked me to wait for him after I was done so he could finish a few things. He invited me into his office, but after what happened there last time, I'm just not ready. I'm too tired to deal with romance.

I'm sitting at my desk in the muggy paralegal's room—which is empty as it's nearly noon. I'm hopelessly tossing jelly beans into JR's flower vase (I have the world's worst aim). It's a mindless activity. But I need something to occupy my mind and hands. Because what happened is on instant replay in my head and I want to turn it off.

The door at the end of the room opens. I jump up, on edge.

"Just me." Bennett comes in slowly, giving my racing heart a moment to calm down.

"Sorry. Post-attempted murder jitters I guess."

"Hey, don't worry. It's over now. Over."

I nod and rub my arms. He's right. My mind knows that. My body doesn't. The little shivers start up again.

He tries to bring my focus back to him. "The report's been filed. Alec's in the dungeon, enjoying a delicious meal served up by Golem X. I hear he's trying a new rat claw soup out tonight."

"Sounds amazing," I force a smile. "Too bad I'm gonna miss it."

Bennett smiles down at me and I feel a flutter. I smile wider. Soaking up his big green eyes. There are little flecks of amber in the green. I focus on those. It helps me calm down.

"Thank you."

"For what?"

"Coming to help me."

He chuckles. "I don't know how much help you really needed. You wrestled the murder weapon away from him and locked him in the hall."

"Um … you didn't watch the video yet?" I bite my lip.

"What? No. We haven't had time."

"Well. That's not really what happened. You guys all just kind of assumed that. And I kinda thought the important part of the story was his confession."

I see him tense. "Okay. What happened?"

"I kinda, sorta think I might have figured out my powers."

"I'm listening."

"Okay. Um. Forewarning. You probably won't like this." I watch his eyes darken. And it's scary and sexy at the same time.

"Why won't I like it?"

"Maybe you should sit."

"Maybe you should talk."

"Okay. Okay. So, I get home. And Alec's sitting on my couch. With that knife."

"And I panicked. Froze up. Next thing I know, he had it at my neck."

Bennett groans. "I don't know if I can hear this."

"But then I had a moment. Like of clarity. Or something."

"Okay?"

"I told him to get lost."

Bennett just stares at me, uncomprehending.

I spin around and swipe the jellybeans off my desk. I prop the bag up on my palm for him to see.

"Bennett, I've lost my jellybeans." The bag disappears.

A grin starts to form at the corner of his mouth. "So he..."

"Disappeared. Into the hall."

"I'm glad."

"Me too."

Our eyes get caught up in a mush-filled staring contest.

He reaches down and grabs my hand, slowly, making sure I'm okay with it. His hand is scalding. But I love it. I squeeze his fingers.

Apparently, that's the signal for full-steam ahead because suddenly his other hand is on my waist and his lips are on mine. And oh ... if I thought a kiss was hot before ...

We pull away for a quick breath. I lean into him, on my tippy toes. My lips brush his ear. "Careful. You'll melt your badge if you let this go too far."

He growls. "Worth it." And the next kiss totally is.

But you know me. I can't help but ruin a moment. So, when we break, panting and heated, I say, "Bennett, you've lost your boxers."

He smacks my butt. I giggle.

"Well, let's go search my house to find them."

So we do. And that search takes a very, very long time.

GOLEM BUZZ SLIDES ME ANOTHER DARK AND STORMY, MY third. JR steals it and takes a sip.

We're at the bar at Wanda's Brews. It's pretty empty since we snuck out early on my first day back at the office. To celebrate. Life and stuff. I wish Jacob was here with us, but he left me a voicemail that he was leaving town for awhile. Can't say I blame him. He has to get things sorted out.

For once, I feel like my life has sorted itself out nicely. Very nicely. I could have done with skipping the whole murder accusation and near-death thing, but hey. Ben's been trying very hard to help me forget. Sometimes he even makes me forget my own name.

"Mmm, another round for me too, please," JR bats her eyes. As if that could affect a golem.

"I'll take my well-earned drink back, thanks." I tug it out of her hands and take a rather unladylike gulp. "Never again." I lift my hands in a two fingered salute, to start off the swear JR insists helped her curb her addiction to gummy bears.

"I vow to never again go alone into a construction site."

"And..." she prompts.

"And never again to try and play detective."

"And..." she laser eyes me as I take another drink. This is the part of the swear I don't really want to say.

JR pinches my leg.

"Ow! Okay. Okay. I vow to never again kiss a vampire." I recite it dully. "But I'm still looking."

"From afar. Very very afar."

I sigh. "From afar."

"I don't get it. Bennett's good for you."

"I know," I grab a strand of hair and curl it. I can't help the little blush that spreads. "But what if it doesn't—"

Her hand smashes my lips, blocking the words I'm about to say. I'm in shock as she leans forward and says, "We have learned that your words have consequences, little missy. You will make another vow. Repeat after me. I will never again sabotage my relationship with that steamy, panty-melting, mouthwatering dragon-man."

My jaw drops. "You did not just call my guy panty-melting."

She winks. "A good girl's allowed to be naughty every now and then. And guess what? You just called him your guy."

I smack her arm. "Stop it."

She laughs. I join her. We finish our drinks and get a nice buzz. She's about to text a Broomer when I dig through my purse.

"Gah! I lost my keys! I must have left them in my desk."

She smacks her forehead. "Ly-ly, will you never learn?"

"What?"

"Why couldn't you say, 'Dang, my keys must have dropped on the floor two inches below my feet?' Now we have to go back there."

"I could try it now."

She raises an eyebrow. I say the words, but the keys don't appear.

"So apparently, it's a one-shot deal. Dang it. Sorry. The key thing is habit."

She sighs. "Come on. I'll go with you. If Arnold's gonna call us out for ditching, it's better to get called out together."

I lean on her shoulder as we walk down the road, back to the marble exterior of the Courthouse.

"You're the best," I tell her sincerely.

"Takes one to know one," she replies.

I smile and pull away, so we can head up the steps. As I do, I realize the alcohol is really starting to hit my system.

The doors above us fly open and Luke storms out. He looks ticked.

"Why hellooooooo," I say, in a faux British accent. "Cheerio. Top of the mornin' love."

Luke stops. His eyes widen. When he realizes I'm tipsy, a predatory smile emerges. "Well, hello, gorgeous."

I jerk my head at the courthouse. "What were you doing in there?"

He comes closer. JR puts a protective arm around me. He acknowledges her and stops a respectful distance away. See? Why does she think he's so bad?

"Your little friend keeps trying to pin me down."

"Bennett? For what?" What could Ben possibly have against him now?

"This and that."

"It's cause you're eye candy." That did not just come out of my mouth. No. I look in horror at JR. Her look confirms it. That totally just came out of my mouth. Cringe. I'm an idiot.

Luke doesn't seem to mind. His smile grows. "Don't worry about me. I won't let a guy like that pin anything on me. If you, however, should ever want to pin me down … I'd love to be at your mercy."

"You did not just say that!" I am in awe. That might be the cheesiest, most porntastic thing anyone's said to me, ever.

"Ew. He totally did." JR is clearly disgusted.

But by Luke's smile, he can tell I'm not.

"She's dating the dragon," JR says coldly.

Immediately, Luke sobers up. "Well, if that isn't the worst news of my night."

"Worse than being arrested?" I ask.

He winks. "You ladies better get inside. Dawn's coming." He tips an imaginary hat at us and strolls down the steps, suddenly chipper.

I turn to JR as he disappears. "I don't get it. Why's he happy?"

She rolls her eyes and helps me up the rest of the stairs, which are swerving a little. "If you're gonna be with Bennett, you have to stop flirting with him."

"But …I didn't mean to."

"Yes, I know. You're buzzed. Which is why I'm giving you a pass. But you need to stay away from that guy. He's bad news."

We get to the elevator and get in.

"You're gonna have to help me be good."

"I will."

"Swear it."

She holds up two fingers. I nod.

The doors ding open. "Okay, operation sneaky keys. Here we go!" I stumble out of the elevator and get down on my hands and knees. I crawl past Bella's desk. She's on the phone and stops talking mid-sentence to stare at me.

"Shhhh," I hold a finger to my lips. I point at Arnold, who's waddling across the far end of the room. Then I make a slashing motion across my throat. I crawl to my desk, surprised to see JR's shoes. She's leaning against my desk, my keys in her hand.

"Get down or he'll see you!" I grab her hand.

"Geez, you're more gone than I thought. Ly-ly, we work in a room full of werewolves. Pack-mind, remember?"

I sit back on my heels as it comes back to me. "Oh. Oh yeah."

I start to get up, and realize my shins are covered in were-fur. "Dang it all!"

"Do you have a problem Ms. Fox?"

I wince. Arnold. I slowly turn around, not sure how to minimize the damage.

"It's your first day back."

"Yessir."

"So, I was going to wait to do this until tomorrow. But, seeing as we can't stand each other and you snuck out early today—you've been transferred."

"I. What?" Now the room is not only spinning, it's cartwheeling. My world is upside down.

"Yes. *Some* people here think that you sniffing around in dark corners shows promise, rather than a reluctance to do work." His tone makes it very clear he was not in agreement with *some* people.

"She's being transferred where?" JR butts in, as I'm still unable to form a coherent sentence.

"Felony investigations."

I turn to JR, wide-eyed. "Bennett's gonna be my boss?"

Gulp.

PREVIEW OF BOOK 2 - ENCHANTED EXECUTION

Ever met a sadist? Like a true, honest-to-God torturer? Join the Tres Lunas Police and Investigation Academy, because apparently that's where evil people work.

And apparently, I was stupid enough to sign up. Which is why I'm here, under the eye of a sadist, doing push-ups. At the freaking crack of sunset.

Yup. My hometown isn't just a haven for magical creatures in So. Cal. It's apparently a place for enchanted torment. Damn! That sounds like a dirty strip-club name. Enchanted Torment ... better not tell Tabby that name. I can just see my friend, a tiny seventy-year-old crystal-ball wielding peeper, throwing her life savings into a club like that. Complete with male were-animal strippers ... I imagine Tabby, my elderly neighbor Mrs. Snow, and their bunco group howling and dancing near the stage. I have to suck down a laugh.

Eff. My wandering brain has stopped my muscles. And the boss has noticed. Lyon Fox, get it together!

I glare at Diego Flores, the commander who is currently eying my stalled push-ups with a lip curled in disgust. Uncurl that lip, Mr. Flores. These biceps weren't trained from the age of three to embrace pain like yours.

I hate Diego (whose nickname by the way, is ironically, Flowers) with a passion that rivals my hatred for all things spicy. I list spicy things as I shake through the last few push-ups of the night.

Cumin, better than Flowers.

Tabasco, nicer than Flowers.

Ghost peppers, as evil as Flowers.

I fall to the mat, not even caring that it's been the site of many a sweaty man's nethers during our wrestling matches. My blonde hair splays out and I close my baby blues, cursing myself for thinking that becoming an investigator was a good idea. It's just five more months. Just five more months ... I don't think five months has felt this long since I was a kid. And it's only five months of half nights. I spend five hours a night at the Academy and five more at the office training on paperwork. I'm a month in. Just five to go.

Unfortunately, the workout is the first two hours every night at the Academy.

I open my eyes to peek at the clock on the wall of the gym. We haven't hit the two-hour mark tonight. Gah!

Flowers—I seriously think he must have some demon blood in there somewhere, though officially he's a tiger-shifter—leans over me and whispers, "One more, Fox."

My arms tremble as I force my body into position. I hiss through my teeth. "I hate you." But I do it.

"Way to push through," he slaps me on the butt with a towel before moving off to torture someone else.

The room goes hazy for a second and I think I've died. If he's killed me, I'm totally going ghost and haunting his toned abs. Literally. I think I'll pop my head through his stomach and start talking at strategic moments. I smile as I picture ruining every date he'll ever have.

Seena and Becca, two other Academy recruits, haul me up so we can go jump over some tires. You know, because I see the police doing that every day. Job essential. Obviously. I've tried to bring up my theory that if we want real-world skills we should practice napping in cars, but Flowers didn't appreciate my insight.

Flowers lines us up so we're three across and blows a whistle like it's kindergarten gym time. "When the person in front of you is three tires ahead, you start. First row. Go!"

I'm toward the back, so I get a breather. Thank goodness.

Seena lines up next to me. He's a Persian shifter. Haven't asked him what kind yet. We've bonded over our hatred of the first two hours of the day. He's in this thing because he's some kind of genius analyst who wants a legal reason to hack computers and outsmart other nerds. And apparently he got bored over at LAPD because—and I quote— "Humans just don't know how to be as devious. We've had centuries more practice." He thinks working as an investigator in Tres Lunas will be more interesting than his last job. Only problem? Every investigator is required to go through the Academy.

"Damn initiation rituals," Seena moans as he rubs his shoulder.

I envy his ability to curse the moment aloud. My fairy mother thought cursing was a nasty habit of mine when I was a teenager. So, what'd she do? Hired a witch to curse me with a cursing curse. Meaning I can't curse aloud. Ever. I try to make up for it internally. But it's not really the same. The best I can do is spit out some texty curses, or some lamebrain options like—

"It's total horse puckey." I nod fervently, agreeing with Seena.

Becca lines up on my other side and grins. She's an effervescent and cheerful sprite, whom I befriended against all odds. Normally I don't like girls as bubbly as soda pop.

But there's something about her that's just so damn lovable. Maybe it's the fact that she's got one of those perfect heart faces with eternally pinchable cheeks.

"The fun team is ready to rock!" She crosses her eyes and does a devil sign with her hands.

Screech! Our turn.

Seena puffs as he runs the tires next to me. "Okay. You ready? Persian insult … of the day: zahré mar. It means … poison of the snake. Like bullshit—"

"How are those even … equivalent?" Becca asks, words punctuated by hard breathing. "I mean … bullshit stinks. Gross. But snake poison? Not … the same level. Death. Totally illogical."

"They both suck … to step on?" Seena offers. "I don't decide translations. I'm just here … to expand your vocab."

"Well, that translation's … zahré mar," Becca retorts.

"Too busy dying … to learn! … Zahré mar!" I retort, as my legs catch on fire. Seena's been on this kick to help me expand my cursing abilities. Apparently, my mom's curse doesn't pick up on Persian words.

"Good!" Seena pants. "Both proper uses."

"Whoop!" Becca loses her balance and grabs my arm. I trip, tumbling face first into Seena. He falls forward into the cadet in front of him, and we create a domino effect, effectively felling those in front of us.

Screech!

Flowers blows on his whistle. As if that'll do anything to stop the disaster.

"Okay dimwits. Since tires are too complicated, let's do laps." His glare at our trio clearly spells out who's responsible for the laps. Thanks man. As if this hazing thing wasn't enough. Like tripping was Becca's fault? She's barely five feet! Those tires are almost as high as her knees.

We groan, detangle, and run laps. And laps. And laps.

Until we finally hit that blessed two-hour mark.

But we don't get to collapse. Nope. Shower? Nope. We get to move on to practicing spells.

I groan.

I'm a mutt. My mom has some strange amalgamation of fairy blood—white, fall, flower… you name it, it's in her gene pool. It's been diluted over the centuries by other creatures and humans too. My dad? Full human. So, though I'm fairy enough to have been born with a blue jewel in my chin and black toenails, magic ain't my game, yo. That's my fairy gangster voice. It's what I used to use whenever I was pretending to be standoffish when I'd visit my mother beyond the Veil. It totally worked. Made all the powerful fairies back right off. Yeah. I wish.

I do have two minuscule powers. The first is—you guessed it (because every magical creature's got it)—quick healing. Maybe I'd feel better about this one if I was a were-animal and prone to fights for alpha status. Or if I was a troll who just liked to fight. But I'm basically a reading-and-junk-food-obsessed shut in. So that power's never been all that good to me. (I've totally suppressed the memories of the time I was attacked by a crazy vampire and later accused of her murder. So not bringing it up.) My other lamebrain power is ... wait for it. Losing things. Yup. That's me. Need something lost? I can do it for you.

Flowers is under some delusion that I can learn to enhance my power. Ha. Yeah. I can see that being so useful as an investigator. Let me help you lose your keys. No keys? How about your kid?

I rub a tired hand over my face. I need to tamp it down. And focus. Or I'm not gonna make any 'progress' and I'll be on Flower's shit list. The bottom three recruits each night get tasked with some awful assignment. And he's clearly gunning for my little trio since we caused the pileup tonight.

I line up near Becca and grab a couple of yoga blocks. I'm supposed to try to 'lose them' to a specific location.

I stare at my block. Concentrate. Visualize. Like all the self-help spell books say to do. "I've lost my yoga block in the men's locker room." The block disappears.

But does it go to the men's locker room? Of course not. Instead, it reappears just above Flowers head.

Bonk.

My classmates all laugh. I can't help it. I laugh. He didn't even see it coming.

But I stop laughing when he marches right over to me.

"Fox!"

"Yessir."

"I'm going to assume that was a mistake."

"Yes, sir, it was."

"Please demonstrate your spell."

I try not to let my hands shake as Flowers glares at me. I don't know where he learned to glare like that, but he's got a good one. It's got me ready to cry and run at the same time. Not to mention the fact that every eye in the gym is now about to watch me and my lame powers. I'd hoped to fly under the radar through the Academy. No such luck.

I grab a new block. I stare at it, willing it to behave.

"I've lost my yoga block in the men's locker room."

Bonk.

This time the block bonks Seena on the head.

"Hey!" Seena throws the block at me and misses.

Flowers lips don't even twitch. I wonder if he's secretly a cyborg.

"You're not focusing." He steps closer and shoves a new block into my arms.

Right now, all I can focus on is his steely-eyed glare. My BFF might think he was sexy. JR's got a thing for strong Latino men. But Flowers is frickin' intense. In a scary way.

I take a slow deep breath. Don't tempt the monster.

"Stop trying to be a clown. Send that block somewhere serious."

"Like your office? That's about the most serious room in the building." Dammit! That just slipped out.

A middle-school-like chorus of "Oooooooh," sounds off around us.

A deep breath. That's his only reaction. A deep breath. This guy's got nerves of steel. I can't help admire that a little. Until he leans in. Then I'm scared again.

"Fill my office with blocks, Fox. Until you do, you've earned a permanent spot on my list."

Mother eff. Frickin' idiot. I'm so stupid.

He saunters off, all cool confidence. I drop my block and ball my free hands into fists to keep myself from throwing the block at him.

Seena comes over and pats me on the head. "Don't worry, Lyon. I'm sure it'll only be the worst thing possible short of death." His brown eyes glitter in amusement.

I smack him in the stomach.

Seena takes it like a computer nerd and crumples to the floor. I feel slightly better for being mean. Pecking order right? Until he winks up at me and hops to his feet. Dammit! Faker!

Becca bumps my shoulder from the other side. "Meow. Who's that?" She not-so-subtly jerks her head toward the double doors of the gym.

"Frick. Frick. Frick." I pull her in front of me.

"That's the double ex," Seena whispers across me as I try to use the two of them as a human shield.

"Is that a porn reference? God, I hope he's on film naked somewhere," Becca giggles.

I smack her arm. "No. That's my ex."

"What's double ex mean then?"

Seena raises an eyebrow as Bennett walks our way. "It means Ly-Ly was stupid enough to break up with this guy twice."

"No!" Becca turns to me. "Say it isn't true?"

I duck further behind Seena, not giving up the ruse, though Bennett's eyes are locked on mine.

Black hair, piercing green eyes, chiseled jaw. A dragon-shifter heartthrob. That I told I needed a break. Because... I stare at his eyes. He's staring back so intensely that I have a hard time remembering why we're on a break.

Becca smacks me. "You broke up with that?"

Her smack snaps me out of the spell his eyes have put on me.

"Yup."

My eyes slip to Bennett's pecs, outlined in detail by the wife-beater he's wearing. He's also got on official Tres Lunas Investigation sweats. He must be here for a workout. My mind slips back to the workouts he used to give me in the bedroom. And suddenly, I'm sweating for a reason that has nothing to do with my aching muscles.

"Are you crazy?" Becca stage whispers.

"Maybe," I reply.

Bennett reaches us and gives respectful nods to Seena and Becca.

"Ms. Fox. Can I have a word?"

Shit. He's sought me out and is being formal. This can't be good.

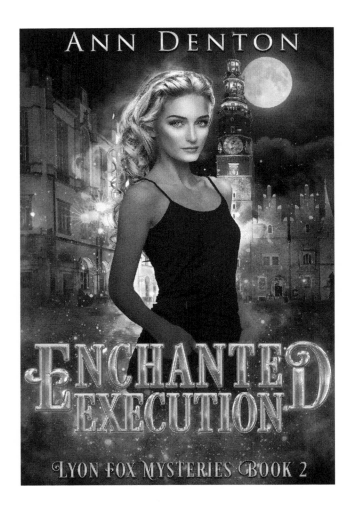

Enchanted Execution - The Lyon Fox Mysteries Book 2 is available now at Amazon!

A PERSONAL NOTE FROM LYON FOX

Hey!

So, we're like friends now, right? Not like secret friends. But like friends who talk and post on Facebook for each other's birthdays and stuff, right? (Mine's October 16th.) Because I totally just told you like tons of personal stuff. And it would be really embarrassing if you turned me down after that.

Ouch! Gah, the writer's poking me to tell you about real-life moments from the book.

Um, they are all true to *my* life. But apparently *my* life doesn't count. Because I'm a fictional character. What B.S. Hello? Did you not feel my fear when I thought I was going down for that Georgina thing? What's more real than that?

Apparently, these things:

1. There was actually a first date at an Indian restaurant where the bathroom door was locked and dine and ditch looked like a possibility.

2. A version of Squirts.

3. There is a woman who's ditzy enough to only read coloring

books. Yeah, it's mean. But I bet you know one, too.

Ugh. And now, as if things aren't bad enough, she wants me to tell you that I write the emails for the reader group. WHAT? No. I refuse. I already have a new job. And apparently, it's harder to be a cop than an attorney because I have to go to the Academy and train.

B.S. I am not writing you any letters. (Totally writing you letters) FUDGING FRICK! She's taking over my fingers. Make this stop. Don't one-click books 2 or 3. Not worth it.

Whoa. Hold up. She's saying if I suck at advertising, she's gonna kill me off. Call the cops! Don't let her kill me! Shoot. Shoot. Okay. Fine. Please—pretty please tell your friends about me and how awesome I am. Tell that weird co-worker who has no social skills and all the people on Amazon.

Ignore this crazy bee of an author's threats and just tell me you love me. Leave a review. Because, like, how else am I gonna know about your love? I only exist in words. So, anything that's not written down technically doesn't exist for me.

Peace out-

Ly

AFTERWORD

Thank you so much for reading! You are amazing, and you are the reason I can keep dreaming up beautiful worlds. If you liked this book, please leave an Amazon review and tell your friends!

Your reviews and recommendations keep me pumped up as I write the next book. So, thanks!

ACKNOWLEDGMENTS

Big thanks to the following people:

The hub. Obviously. For being awesome and pushing me to pursue this dream.

Raven, Ivy, Mia, Aubry, S, Janie, Christine, Rebecca, Lacey, Josephine, Misti, Kezi, and everyone else who provided feedback or love to Lyon. I couldn't have done it without you.

The kiddos. Thanks for the nights you went to sleep early.

OTHER BOOKS BY ANN DENTON

The Lyon Fox Mysteries

My fun urban fantasy series is full of mystery and laughter with a fade-to-black romance.

Magical Murder - Book 1

Enchanted Execution - Book 2

Supernatural Sleep - Book 3

Hexed Hit - Book 4

Tangled Crowns Series

My first reverse harem series is the Tangled Crowns series. It's a medieval fantasy with a bully romance feel in the first book. It's medium burn.

Knightfall - Book 1

MidKnight - Book 2

Knight's End - Book 3

Lotto Love Series

My second reverse harem series is the Lotto Love series. Its a rom-com reverse harem with a private island, lottery money, and tons of handsome men. It's medium burn.

Lotto Men - Book 1

Lotto Trouble - Book 2

Jewel's Cafe Series

Jewel's Cafe is a series of stand-alone reverse harem novels each written by a different author. My book is Ruby, the sixth title in the twelve book series. Ruby is about a clumsy angel who doesn't "get" humans, and the tech demon and two computer nerds determined to help her. It's medium burn.

Ruby - A Reverse Harem Romance

Timebend

If you're in the mood for more intrigue, check out my Postapocalyptic Thriller series.

Melt - Book 1

Burn - Book 2

CONNECT AND GET SNEAK PEEKS

If you like to read exclusive snippets from different characters, make predictions with other readers, see my inspiration for books, or just come hang and be yourself, I have a Facebook reader group.

Go Here to Join Ann Denton's Reader Group:

https://www.facebook.com/
groups/AnnDentonReaderGroup/

ABOUT ME

I'm a Virgo. I've driven around town finding landmarks based on a friend's dream. And, I'm addicted to dark chocolate bars with espresso. I have a hubster who encourages my crazy pants ways. I have two amazing little humans who look up to me right now, but won't for long because I'm very short.

I love the arts: painting, theatre, and reading. I have an undergrad degree in Playwriting and a grad degree in Theatre History. Socrates rocks my socks.

I'm an INTJ. If you've never taken a Meyers Briggs personality test, I recommend them.

I would love to talk to you about the book. Yes you. You can ask me questions on Facebook. If you sign up for my newsletter on my website, I'll email you about upcoming books.

Ann@AnnDenton.com

www.AnnDenton.com

Made in the USA
Middletown, DE
01 August 2022